THE ANVANTARAS

DEBJIT CHATTERJEE

I would like to thank Notion Press and everyone who has been a part of this journey.

Writing a book is not easy and breezy, but the experience of unravelling something beyond the standard reality around us is both exciting and daunting in the same breath. I would like to thank those who willingly chose to sacrifice their time and energy to ensure I embark on this endeavour uninterrupted

Lastly, I would like to thank those who felt I was being too ambitious to try something like this, and more definitely take it to closure, it was due to them I had to finish.

Contents

Preface

It all began with the evolution about three hundred thousand years ago from homo sapiens to humans and then our evolution is believed to have stopped. But what if this evolution never stopped? What if the human race continued to evolve into super intelligent and powerful beings – their existence hidden as secret of the Anvantaras.

The truth is, the Anvantaras have been living among for millenniums concealing their original identities. Through out history though, the Anvantaras revealed themselves to help humans in times of great need...though their deeds were often camouflaged as mythologies or folklore.. And, they wisely chose not to contest this when they were called Gods. So, what does this make Odin, Zeus, Rama, Shiva, Jesus...- mere mythological characters or were they Anvantaras too?

I

The new dawn

Mount Song, Henan Province, China

Tucked away quietly in the snowy lap of Songshan mountains, the Shaolin Temple rose like a timeless relic. This oldest and perhaps the greatest martial arts institutions in the world and unarguably, was one of the best guarded ones. Its shimmering golden gate, perched atop a rather daunting flight of uneven stone steps, overlooking the vast, misty valleys and dense forests beneath. A warm fragrance of incense sticks lingered in cold, mountain air. This house of learning and power drew many a silent spectator every day, even the locals would stand in the shadows of this temple, enthralled by its glory and prowess. They would marvel at the grandeur, but would be intimidated to step foot into that mystical world.

But not everyone came as a silent visitor. In the faint light of the dawn, when a group of imposing figures commenced their ascent, they had a complete different objective- their long black linen hooded robes contrasting against the sheer whiteness of the snowy mountains.

The way they went about the countless flights of stairs seemed strangely synchronized- not the faintest sound of the gravel underfoot, no sign of fatigue or endurance. It's almost as if they were in a rush, yet for a purpose far beyond the limits of any ordinary traveler.

The tallest of the cloaked figures, exuding an quiet air of authority, stepped forward. His broad frame appeared to be blocking the icy winds that swirled around the mountain peak. He stretched his veiny arms to ring the heavy bronze bell next to the delicately carved brown dragon in the center of the golden gate.

Two armed, middle-aged Shaolin guards dressed in orange robes emerged.

Their hands rested calmly on the hilts of their weapons and their eyes impervious to the masked faces of the visitors; Shaolin wasn't a stranger to secrets! In fact, the number of secrets it had guarded all these years could have blown the world, had they ever been unleashed.

The leader, his face obscured beneath the shadow of his hood, bent slightly and greeted respectfully, his voice deep and steady.

"What is your purpose, Mister?" One of the guards asked. His stance was one of unyielding authority, but there was no hostility in his voice.

"We wish to meet Master Hung" The leader replied, his words, measured and calm.

The guard's expression didn't shift. "Master Hung is meditating" He said flatly. "He sees no one"

The man inclined his head slightly, undeterred. "We can wait" He replied firmly.

The two guards exchanged a brief glance, their weathered faces giving no emotion away. The biting mountain winds howled as the guards deliberated, their unspoken exchange leading to a silent standoff, as the cloaked figures waited patiently.

"Mister, I told you, Master Hung sees no one, leave now", one of older guards repeated what seemed like an age of silence. He swiftly leaned forward to close the gate, but instead was hurled backwards across the sprawling courtyard, landing in a heap near the temple's main entrance. The other guard, the stockier and seemingly slightly older, didn't make any attempt to fight. He didn't lunge forward or even drew his weapon. He simply stepped back a few yards, reached into his orange robes and pulled out a long, silver whistle. Raising it to his thin lips, he blew it with all his might. The piercing sound split the air, cutting through the wintery night like a relentless alarm.

Moments later, the ground trembled as a thunderous stampede erupted from the shadows- some three hundred Lusaka Warriors had formed an impenetrable wall between those masked intruders and the Shaolin.

These were no ordinary soldiers- they were legends.

The Lusaka Warriors were the most dreaded fighting force in the East. The stories of their valor and unmatched glory echoed through centuries. During the mid-thirteenth century, when the Japanese Emperor in a devious plan to invade China had sent a troop of two thousand of his best Samurai Warriors, the Chinese Emperor sent just a hundred and fifty of his elite Lusaka Warriors to counter the Japanese soldiers. Entire China stood stunned at his decision, they questioned him, blamed him, even called him crazy and whimsical, for the glory of the Samurais was unparalleled in the East, but the Chinese Emperor was unnerved. When the battle finally concluded, three major islands of the Japanese archipelago had been captured by the Lusaka Warrior, and what was left of the fierce Samurais, was just their legend.

But somehow the masked men remained eerily calm. They stood still like stone statues, their hands casually placed on the hilt of the weapons. The Lusaka warriors though didn't care for warnings.

But followed next was unthinkable. Their movements were unlike what the Lusaka Warriors had ever witnessed. They gripped their swords in a strange way between their thumb and index finger, as it was an extension of their very beings. Their speed and power defied human capability, swinging like the rotating blades of a windmill, the masked men slashed through every Lusaka warrior that came in contact of those blazing swords, as if the Chinese armor the warrior wore and the weapons they wielded were made of paper. The clash of steel overpowered even the loud winds howling through the courtyard. Punctuated by cries of pain and sickening thuds of bodies hitting the ground, in a matter of minutes, the great wall of Lusaka Warriors had been infiltrated- the Shaolin men in action were rendered dead or writhing in agony.

And yet, the masked men seemed untouched by the chaos they had unleashed. Their movement mechanical yet graceful, their strength and precision otherwordly. Nobody knew where these masked men came from, or what they wanted, except that their uncanny fighting skills seemed far superior and their strength almost supernatural.

"Enough!"

A voice rang sharp and commanding, pierced through the silence of death that had just preceded.

A rather short man stood staring from the far end of the courtyard, his silhouette illuminated by the dim light of the rising sun. His appearance was striking; a round face like a ripened watermelon, crowned by a long white moustache that curved downwards. His nose neither long, nor short but just flat and unremarkable, yet his piercing gaze held authority. In his hand, he clutched a thick golden staff, etched with intricate carvings that shimmered faintly in the morning light.

The tall leader of the masked men slowly threw back his hood, revealing his imposing figure. "Please accept Tvashar's greetings, Oh the Great Nera Hung", he said in his usual calm tone.

Tvashtar was well over seven feet, an intimidating giant whose presence commanded both awe and unease. His head was mostly shaved except for thick patch of dark grey hair at the center of his skull. Tvashtar was perfect for a prized wrestler – taut muscles, blue veins, and large steady hands. A coiled python tattoo snaked up his neck, its head resting just below his jaws, its eyes inked in a way that made it look alive. His eyes were oceanic green and fierce with intensity, and a deep sword scar ran from his left temple to his square jaw, a testament to the countless battles he had braved. There was a strange blend of intrigue and terror, a man whose appearance seemed to dare anyone to oppose him.

"Tvashtar!" Master Hung froze in his place. His knuckles tightened around his staff, though his face showed fear, but his voice exuded shock. Of all places, he had never expected Tvashtar at Shaolin, although he was warned about the possibility. After all, how could Tvashtar find him at Shaolin? China was so far, so unrelated from the epicenter of these dark forces.

Tvashtar's spanned across the courtyard, where the broken bodies of Lusaka Warriors lay scattered. Blood stained the scared stones of the temple's steps, and the air was still heavy with the smell of iron and blood. "Forgive me for all the mess, Nera Hung," Tvashtar sighed softly, his tone had a hint of lightness, as if savoring the chaos he had just rendered. "Your men left me no Bahadurce!"

"My men only did their duty" Master Hung replied, steadying his voice. His gaze didn't waver as he stared at the towering figure before him "Tell me Tvashtar, why do you seek me?"

Tvashtar's lips curled into faint, ominous smile, "Oh the great Nera Hung! Nothing escapes your eyes and you still want the answer". His tone carried a low growl, like a predator toying with its prey.

Master Hung looked away, his expressions betrayed the stoic face he had been putting up.

"I seek the *Pud,*" Tvashtar declared, "the eternal drink of power and glory"

Master Hung's expression hardened at once. He gripped his staff tighter. "That's impossible" He said firmly, "you know it doesn't exist, it's a myth, Tvashtar"

Tvashtar's smile faded, a dangerous glint appeared in eyes. "It may be a myth for the humans" He snarled, his tone menacing. "But, we both know the truth"

"But I do not have the *Pud,* Tvashtar" Master Hung insisted. His voice unyielding.

Tvashtar turned to his trusted military chief General Kofi Raj, a man who stood slightly closer to Tvashtar as against the rest of the masked men. The grey-haired General was a figure of quiet strength and intellect, rumored to be fluent in almost every language in the world.

"What does the book say, General?" Tvashtar looked at his Military Chief with dark anticipation

"Your Highness, the book says... *'I looked at the sun and wished it was mine...Now that it is in my palms, I wonder where is the shine?'*" General Kofi Raj spelled out the riddle, pondering over its words, staring deep into a small book in his palm. He paused for a few long seconds, studying the words closely, then he looked up at Tvashtar abruptly. "I think the handle of the staff holds the glass, His Highness" he said softly, his tone deliberate and measured.

Tvashtar's eyes snapped to the golden staff in Master Hung's hands. "Grab the staff" King Tvashtar ordered, his voice stern. Two men lurched at Master Hung. Their movements swift and predatory.

Master Hung's agility was astonishing for his age. He moved slightly backwards and pressed his staff into the first man's chest; the man wobbled and stumbled down the stairs. The other attacker too, flinched for a second, taken aback by the ferocity of the old master's attack. Recovering fast, he swung his long sword at Master Hung, the Little Master ducked. Swinging his entire weight on the staff, Master Hung threw both his legs, catching the attacker between his stomach and the groin, the man bellowed in pain.

Tvashtar's men were stunned by the swiftness and power of this sudden attack. This fight had not gone according to their plan. The masked intruders usually invincible in their confidence had found an adversary par excellence.

"How did you forget Tvashtar, I am also a Anvantara" Master Hung jeered.

Tvashtar furiously threw back his cloak. ""So be it...you obnoxious old man". His bulging biceps gleamed in the moonlight. He wasn't accustomed to his men meeting such consequences.

Master Hung made the first move. He swirled his staff at Tvashtar with a deadly precision, but the young leader anticipating the strike, blocked it swiftly with his sword. The collision of the staff and the sword created a resonance that even the thick walls of Shaolin shuddered to this monumental clash. It was if two elephants had locked their trunks in battle so fierce, so wild that even nature couldn't dare to intervene - the sword against the staff, age against agility and finesse against ferocity. The little master wasn't bluffing when said about being a Anvantara. Tvashtar was getting a taste of Master Hung's intense dexterity, every time their weapons clashed or the fists flews, sometimes even Tvashtar simply stood gaping in admiration, and anger. But in the end, the fury and flair of the young leader was far more intense than the skills and experience of Shaolin Supremo. And when at last Tvashtar's blade found its mark, Master Hung fell down, wounded gravely.

His words came out slow, ragged gasps *"Tvashtar, a small flower in the sand...... alone it will stand, though away from its band, yet out of your hand"* Tvashtar snatched the staff off the old man's blood stained hands, *"The darkness can eclipse the moon and even the star..... yet it's the light of a little candle that even it can't mar"* The wounded master continued, his face wincing with pain, *"For the one, who wrongfully wields the power of Pud ,will soon end up, in a pool of blood"* In fact, the last few words were barely audible as blood clogged his throat. Shaolin wept at the loss of its powerful leader. The temple once a symbol of strength amd wisdom, now felt empty and cold.

"What does the riddle mean General?" Tvashtar continued cleaning the blood stained staff with a handkerchief. Satisfied, he jolted the staff forward, and turned it clockwise, there was a soft click. A very long, narrow glass, the shape of a test tube was carefully fixed inside the thick handle of the staff. The glass of *Pud* dazzled in the moonlight, its ends glistening, and it's content, white and pure as the first raindrop. Cautiously, Tvashtar brought the rim of the glass up to his dark, tobacco-stained lips, "To Eternal Power and Glory."

"His Highness, the master meant that a young Anvantara, born to humans, would be the reason for your death."

Tvashtar's eyes narrowed as he considered the General's words. "Oh, the Great General! Then find me that young Anvantara." His voice filled with cold determination.

==============================XXXXXXXXXXXXXXXXXX==============================

At that very moment, only five thousand kilometers from Shaolin, another storm was brewing.

And, whatever that ice storm touched that night, collapsed like a pack of cards. Huge pine trees weighing over a thousand pounds were uprooted and torn apart like fragile twigs; barks of banyan trees, some as wide as fifty feet, splintered and shattered. Gas stations, houses, stores, almost every structure that had stood in its way crumbled into heaps of rubble and concrete. The village looked as though it had been intentionally erased.

In the aftermath, the devastated residents of Nagvari rushed to the old village hospital, which stood miraculously intact even amidst the storm! This pale, century-old weathered and worn building endured, as if assisted by some divine intervention. But little did anybody know that the hospital's survival held a deeper purpose

A purpose that could defy the wrath of nature itself. A purpose that made this desperate world pin their hopes on two newborns, one a prince and the other coming from poverty. Until that moment, both the boys hadn't even seen the first ray of sun, their lives still cloaked in the darkness of a brooding Himalayan night.

From the shadows of the trees, a voice, hoarse and faint, declared, 'He's born!' His words were interrupted by piercing wails of a newborn, ripped through the night's frightening calm

"But we still can't say which one is *him!*" came a disappointed sigh. From the shadows of the night, her face remained hidden but the silver strands in her flowing light brown hair caught the fleeting glimmers of moonlight, adding an ethereal grace to her.

"What do you mean?" The man looked at his companion, his voice tense.

"It is not just one," There was a chill in her tone, "but two boys who have been born here"

"Two boys?" The man looked puzzled.

"Didn't you hear those two simultaneous cries?"

"But I heard just one" He muttered

"Wait" The lady gripped his arm, and pulling him closer to the hospital, though still in the shadows, "Listen now!"

She was right, there were two cries, both coming from the same direction, "Damn," The man cursed under his breath, the realization dawning upon him. "How do we now know which one of them is *him?*"

==============================XXXXXXXXXXXXXXXXXX==============================

7 years later- 12-Apr (7:30 AM)

The endless sea of emerald, green grass stretched into the horizon, dissolving eventually into pale blue sky. The gentle breeze flowing from the north carried a bite of cold, but it was soothing, almost hypnotic. The boy sprawled on the soft grass, basking in the rare stillness of the moment. Lazily, he stretched his arms. He could afford this luxury, at least he thought so.

The sound came faintly at first, a distant rumble barely discernable over the rustling grass. He brushed if off as a figment of his lazy imagination, part of the dreamy haze the tranquil day had induced. But then, the rthym of the hoof beats grew louder and closer, cutting through the stillness like an ominous dream. He opened his eyes reluctantly, and with even a far greater effort, sat up.

And then he saw it.

A cloaked figure on a horseback emerged from the horizon, riding a brown steed. The rider appeared to be a man from the broad of his shoulders, and he was tall, very tall. His dark linen robe flowing with the wind, his face obscured by a smooth, featureless white mask. He had a strange steadiness to his gait as he dismounted, his piercing gaze fixed on the boy.

The boy froze, his breath caught in his throat. The masked rider stopped just a few feet away, silent, unmoving as if deliberating some unfathomable decision. The stillness was suffocating, a void only filled by the whisper of the breeze and the

boy's racing hear beat. Then, like a lightening, the man pulled out a long thin blade and swung it wildly at the boy'

Parth woke up with a gasp, his body drenched in sweat, his heart pounding furiously against his ribcage. He looked around in panic. The room was dark and silent, but the image of the blade, so vivid, so close, still hung in the air like an unshakeable shadow. This nightmare, it had haunted him for as long as he could remember, a relentless specter that returned without fail, year after year, on the same fateful day.

"Happy Birthday Parth" Dida's warm voice broke the trance as she swept into room and pulled the heavy curtains apart, flooding the space with bright morning light. She sat gently beside her son, a tender smile playing on her lips. Anywhere else in the world, Dida would have been considered attractive, but the heavyset villagers of Nagvari found her slender frame and delicate features frail, almost drought stricken. She had always been this way- lean and graceful. Her bony fingers reached out, brushing away a stray strand of dark hair off Parth' forehead; her son needed a haircut, she noted mentally.

"Are we going somewhere, Ma?" Parth asked curiously, his eyes shifting to the figure in the doorway. His father, Avneesh Anand, had just walked into the room, dressed in his best, blue suit, that only made appearance for special parties or celebrations. The sight unusual enough to raise a question, as Avneesh rarely indulged into such formalities. At forty three, Avneesh looked far older; his weathered face and graying hair betraying the weight of the years. Once dark and thick, his hair had long surrendered to the streaks of grey, brushed back in a half-hearted attempt to make them look tidy. That overdue haircut- costly barely 10 rupees- remained on his ever-growing list of to-dos. There was a time, not so long ago, Avneesh was not like this, he was full of vigor and youthfulness when he married Dida two decades ago. But years since then had passed in a blink – raising four children, being the sole bread winner , and wrestling daily responsibilities had taken their toll. Avneesh didn't even realize how quickly he had aged in his pursuits of meeting the ends.

"We are going to Arjun' birthday", Dida smiled at her husband. Avneesh smiled back at her. For Dida, her life had been painfully monotonous- a cycle of duties and responsibilities that left no room for any indulgence. But she never complained, she loved Avneesh deeply and admired his unwavering dedication to their family. It was not perfect, but it was theirs and she embraced it with grace.

Parth however couldn't hide the resentment bubbling inside him. He hated this routine, this yearly reminder of how his own birthday had become an afterthought. For the past eight years, without fail, the Mehta family had been throwing lavish parties for their son, Arjun- a boy who seemed to have everything. And every year, much to his frustration, Parth found himself sitting at someone else's celebration, a reluctant guest on the very day that was supposed to be his.

He quietly clenched his fist, a wave of bitterness sweeping over him. *Another year, another birthday stolen.*

==============================xxxxxxxxxxxxxxxxxx==========================

Mehta Residence, 12-Apr (11:45 AM)

A warm glow of string lights and the echo of laughter filled the Mehta mansion. Jignesh cleared his throat and tried to raise his voice above the hum of the gathering. "There you are Avneesh. Ladies and gentlemen, for those who may not know, this is Avneesh Anand, my newest senior foreman" He announced with a genial smile, gesturing towards Avneesh, who stood next to him, visibly uncomfortable with the spotlight.

Over two hundred guests erupted in a brief applause, though it quickly faded as back into the clinking of of soft drink glasses and bursts of laughter. This was after all, one of the most awaited parties of the year, and Jignesh Mehta, the wealthiest man in Nagvari never failed to deliver grandeur. An endless spread of appetizers, rivers of soft drinks and unmatched hospitality- always made his parties the talk of the town. But for the Anand family, this year's party was different. It wasn't just another invitation. It marked Avneesh's elevation in the village hierarchy and the recognition for the blood and sweat he had invested in to Jignesh's furniture factory.

As Avneesh offered a humble smile, trying to acknowledge Jignesh's pride with grace, a sudden commotion erupted at the gate. A man, breathless and frantic darted towards Jignesh. "Mr. Mehta, Mr. Mehta Sir"

The voice was enough to freeze the room. Jignesh turned to the man, his calm demeanor masking the unease that was stirred by the visitor. As the headman of Nagvari, he knew such interruptions rarely came without weight. "Joseph" He said. His tone steady, "What is it?"

Joseph, one of the village security volunteers bent over, gasping for breath. A glass of water brought to him, which he downed in one gulp before speaking "Sir, there's been an accident"

For the first time since the tables had been laid that afternoon, the guests actually looked beyond their full plates, and overflowing glasses.

"What kind of accident?" Jignesh asked, his voice still unshaken, though tension in brow betrayed him, "tell me what it is?"

Joseph hesitated. His hands trembled as he clutched the corner of his trousers tightly. "Sir, Karim... Karim Ahmed Sir"

Doctor Iqbal Ahmed, who had been standing near the buffet table froze. His face drained as he pushed his way through the crowd. "Karim? What happened to my boy? He was just just here.... Karimmm?" His frantic voice pierced the silence as he searched for his son among the guests.

"Doctor" Joseph began, still trembling. "Your son, he went to play near the river"

"The river?" Doctor Iqbal stammered. His eyes darting wildly, struggling make sense to the words. "No, no, he was just here. Karim! Karim!"

Joseph stepped back, his face etched with dread, "There was a crocodile in the river, sir. A giant one in the river"

The words sent a ripple of horror through the crowd. Gasps and whispers erupted as the unimaginable reality sunk in. A crocodile? In their river? It was unheard of. Unthinkable.

Doctor Iqbal collapsed to his knees, tears streaming down his face as his worst fear came true. His sobs echoed through the mansion, drowning out the distant music coming from their backyard. Avneesh rushed to his side, gripping his shoulder, but there was no words to console a father who had just lost everything.

Jignesh stood still, his usual composure shattered. "A crocodile" he murmured, his voice barely audible. "In our river?"

"It's impossible" someone muttered from the crowd. "There has never been crocodile in these waters"

Jignesh snapped out of his daze. "Gather all the children, now" He ordered, his tone cutting through the panic. The laughter and joy that had filled this mansion moments ago had vanished in moments. The children blissfully unaware of the tragedy were scooped up by trembling hands and carried away, confused and frightened by the sudden chaos.

The next day, the village awoke to a cloud of mourning. Karim Ahmed's absence was felt everywhere- in the quiet streets, in the hushed tones of neighbors, and more profoundly in the heart of Parth Anand.

For Parth, the loss was crushing. Karim wasn't just a friend; he was his best friend. Now, there was a void in Parth's life, an emptiness that nothing could fill. Not even, the arrival of Arjun Mehta and his sister Sara, who had recently joined the same school.

Initially, Parth despised their presence. Arjun with his privileged life and surname, was an unintentional reminder of reminder of the Parth's own depravity.

But one rainy afternoon, everything changed.

Parth had been struggling with a stubborn kite, its tangled string refusing to obey. Arjun passing by, couldn't resist helping. "You are doing it all wrong." He said, snatching the string. Within minutes the kite soared into the gray sky, its bright magenta color vivid against the gloom.

Reluctantly, Parth muttered. "Thanks"

The next day, Sara was paired with both the boys into math quiz. While Parth grumbled, Arjun's jokes broke the tension, and by the end of it Parth was laughing- a rare sight after that fateful incident with Karim.

The trio began spending the afternoons together. And with time, maybe due to Arjun's relentless persistence to find a friend in school, Parth found himself softening. Despite their differences, Arjun wasn't arrogant or conceited. In fact, he was surprisingly ordinary.

And so, a hesitant friendship forged in the shadow of grief.

II

A Tale to Remember

Parth never felt so trivial before. A house could never get any bigger, not to Parth at least. Its shadows stretching like giant arms engulfing the entire neighborhood around it. This sprawling seventeenth century mansion built by Arjun's great, great grandfather Maheshbhai Mehta loomed large with a faint scent of secrets. . Tales of Maheshbhai's obsession with the house has been whispered over generations. The Mehta family, in the beginning, tried to coax Taos into giving up his whim, but over time, they all resigned. He was so obsessed with house that he vowed to never its walls, spending every waking moment roaming through its cavernous halls until his last day. Some said his ghost still wandered there, bound by his own devotion. Yet, for all its grandeur- its gold-flecked handles, imposing rooms, ancient tapestries and some priceless heirlooms, the mansion held no allure for Parth. He wasn't drawn to its treasures but to what may lie beneath- hidden rooms, trap doors, and secret passages—the curiosities that such houses could evoke.

Seeing his friend's disappointment, Arjun grinned mischievously "Let's go hunting Parth!"

"But what if somebody sees us?" Parth hesitated, remembering Jignesh's stern warning about the woods

"Don't be sissy Parth," Arjun teased. "We will go up north, nobody comes there, besides we have got this" he pulled out a small handgun from his pocket, the black metal glinting wickedly in dim light.

Parth frowned. "A gun would probably make a lot of noise".

Arjun smirked, unscrewing the nozzle. "Relax, its got a silencer, won't make a noise loud enough to even scare a rabbit" He smiled and passed the long detachable pipe fixed at the end of the hand gun to Parth,

Parth studied the long shiny object, its tiny holes catching his curiosity. Before he could protest further, Arjun grabbed his arm and dashed out of the mansion's iron gates.

===============================XXXXXXXXXXXXXXXXXXX=======================

It had been months since the crocodile had been last spotted in the river, yet Jignesh's warning about the beat still lingered. Perhaps, that was why strolling through the woods wasn't tiring or ritualistic, but simply fun and refreshing for the boys – a first in years. The chirping of birds, occasional howls of foxes, ice dripping from the edge of leaves, the muddy path, everything felt new and good. They somehow lost track of time amidst all of this.

But when, several hours of aimless pursuits through the dense forest yielded nothing, the fun started fading into the shadows of boredom, even the sunlight peering through the dense trees above seemed dull now. Left with no better option, the boys disappointedly traced their path back home.

"A rabbit" Arjun's sharp cry came from a distance.

A small brown rabbit nibbled on grass, completely unaware of its stalkers. Parth raised the gun, his hands trembling as aimed. But missed, the rabbit anticipating danger, dashed deeper into the woods.

"Give me that" Arjun grabbed the gun from Parth. His eyes gleaming with excitement while they chased the prey, and bang! The little rodent dropped lifeless to the ground, dead.

Parth cheered, running to retrieve the prize, but this victory was short-lived. When he turned, Arjun was gone.

"Arjun?" Parth's voice cracked as he called out. The woods turned sinisterly still, the earlier hum of life replaced by a haunting silence. "Arjun, where are you?"

No answer.

His heart raced as panic set in. The trees seemed closer now, their twisted branches like fingers poking at him. He ran wildly, his breath coming in short, desperate gasps. Suddenly, as the sun commenced fading in the horizon, he saw a flash of yellow- a jacket Arjun was wearing.

"Arjun" Parth screamed.

But the figure was tumbling, rolling uncontrollably down the green slopes, into the river.

================================XXXXXXXXXXXXXXXXXXX===========================

The cold, bottle green water swirled around Arjun, yet somehow he seemed at ease even. He kicked gently, pushing through the light current, making his way back to the grassy banks.

Parth stood at the edge, his heart pounding with relief heaved a sigh of relief- His friend was swimming back to safety of the banks, unhurt. But, Arjun stopped a few meters from the bank, something was bothering him. He stared at his leg. It seemed like his left leg was caught into something, tangled in a water shrub perhaps! Parth quickly sprinted down the slope to help, but stopped midway. Just inches away from Arjun, floating gently in the water was a bloated, moss colored log, drifting harmlessly in the water. Parth would have dismissed it for a log, had he not noticed its long slanting mouth that met two neat sets of long wicked-looking teeth. That log was moving fast toward Arjun.

The gun was still lying where Arjun had dropped it, but as luck would have it, both the bullets had been spent on the rabbit! Parth knew Arjun badly needed assistance; courage alone wouldn't suffice today for either of them.

"Why is he running? Doesn't he know I am a good swimmer?" Arjun almost groaned to himself (his friend had just sprinted out of the woods, shouting for help). Arjun planted his hands on the sun warmed grassy banks, and heaved up, but he couldn't climb back! Something had pulled him back into the water. It felt strange at first, nothing like what Arjun had ever experienced before. It felt as if a thousand needles had been pierced into his legs, and the grip of those needles was only tightening with every second. And, before Arjun could understand what was happening, he was yanked into the deeper part of the river.

Arjun kicked back in repulse. An apparently clueless Arjun, for the first time saw, what had been long preying on him. It would have been incorrect to say that he wasn't scared; he was indeed, he had heard of what had happened to Karim that fateful day and right now, he was slated for a similar fate. Keeping a cool nerve under such circumstances was therefore too much of a task for a boy his age.

Nervously though, his little fists were flying in natural defense; occasionally catching and often missing the clever beast. But, his last punch, it seems, had hit its mark. The long, ugly, pointed snout of the crocodile was now bleeding. Arjun for the first time felt assured. He understood that with the banks still far and the animal near, he had no way out. With the last bit of strength and spirit left within, Arjun prepared himself-

just as the crocodile pounced on Arjun, his little hands grabbed its heavy jaws. Slipping on countless occasions, his finger slick with blood and water, yet he held on to the crocodile's sticky uneven mouth till it relaxed its body to jerk the boy off and the moment it relaxed, Arjun pulled it's jaws apart, tearing them away from each other like an ordinary piece of paper!

The crocodile fell limp, its body sinking into the darker depth of the river.

Parth's frantic shouts had drawn nearly the entire village to the river banks. That was the day when the entire Nagvari stood an audience to the biggest spectacle of their lives. The story of Arjun and the giant crocodile immortalized him as both the hero and a myth. And, this was perhaps the worst aftermath of that incident.

================================XXXXXXXXXXXXXXXXXXX===========================

III

The Tracker

"Kofi Raj, how long have I known you"? Tvashtar's voice was almost calm now, the disarming tone caught even caught the seasoned General off guard.

"Thirty-five years, your Highness" Kofi Raj answered, unsure where this conversation was leading to.

"Thirty-five years" Tvashtar echoed thoughtfully. He took a deep drag from his pipe and exhaled slowly, the smoke curling at the corner of his lips, spitting fire like a mystical dragon. "In all these years you have served me loyally. But loyalty doesn't mean you know all my secrets. That's how empires collapse, too many people knowing too many things"

Kofi Raj stiffened but nodded, "I would never question your wisdom, your Highness"
\

Tvashtar smiled. "Good, for now then ensure that the Tracker completes his mission. The boy must be eliminated before he becomes a threat. Remember General, even the smallest of ember can ignite a wildfire"

Kofi Raj bowed. "As you command, your Highness"

Tvashtar watched him leave the throne room, while his own mind wandered to the next move. Things were falling in place, and he couldn't afford to take any chances.

Nera Parvati paced the length of her quarters, her mind restless. The task that Nera Brahmashiva had given her and Nera Kashyap was no trivial one. Protecting the boys without revealing themselves was going to be a mammoth task, especially with Tvashtar now on their tail.

"We will need something very solid" Nera Kashyap sighed. He was seated on the small table in her quarter, his fingers steepled as he spoke.

"A plan won't be enough" Nera Parvati replied. "We need to anticipate Tvashtar's every move. And that means finding about this Tracker. If he is as good as they say, our hands will be more than full"

Nera Kashyap nodded. "I will mobilize my people immediately then. In the meantime, let us keep a close eye on the boys, that's our only hope"

Nera Parvati stared out of the windows, her gaze fixed on the distant icy mountains. "Let's pray we are not too late"

Bad news travelled faster, and when Shaolin fell, the whispers of doom loomed large in their world. In no time it was known far and wide: Tvashtar possessed the *Pud*, making him the undisputed leader of the Anvantaras. His shadow stretched over the lands, striking fear into the hearts of many.

But not all.

Far away, hidden among the untouched valleys of earth, there existed a small clan of Anvantaras who were Relatively unperturbed by Tvashtar's rise. To them everything was unfolding as foreseen!

This clan was called "Neras". History has it that some of the wisest and most powerful Anvantaras, chose the path of wisdom and righteousness. These Anvantaras dedicated their lives to ensuring harmony between the humans and Anvantaras. They called themselves the Neras, meaning "the Peacekeepers" in the ancient language.

Standing at heart of the auditorium was Nera Harinath Brahmashiva, the current supreme leader of the Neras. "Nera Hung had died an honorable death, may he rest in peace as we stand here today for his tenth death anniversary", his deep baritone thundered through the giant hall of Gurukule, the foremost institution for Neras, "My dear friends, Nera Hung's sacrifice while on the one hand has shown us, how vulnerable we are to the never-ending quest for power. And, on the other hand, it's a perfect example of character – even the fear of death can't bend a Nera's true duties".

"But, Nera Brahmashiva, if I may interrupt" a frail looking young man standing in the fourth row raised a hesitant hand. He was wearing a horn rimmed glasses that looked too big for his face, "Do you think with the growing power and ambitions of King Tvashtar, a war between us and humans is inevitable?".

Nera Brahmashiva's sharp gaze rested on the young man, "Two things Nera Vashon are of utmost importance". His voice was stern, yet kind, "first, it would never be "us" against humans. It may only be King Tvashtar and "his men" who may take up arms against the humans and mark my words "they too *may*, may not *will* wage a war against humans." Nera Brahmashiva paused, his eyes traveling over his audience, they were all listening, looking at the Nera Supremo with interest, "Second, no matter how strong the rock may be, the river still paves its path. Mother Nature has its balance, and it will correct what has been wrong...." The Nera Supremo had a faint glint in his eyes, "....always" he said softly.

Nera Vashon folded his hands, "please forgive my ignorance, Nera Supremo"

"Thank you Neras. I am sure you will all live for the same virtues that Nera Hung has sacrificed his life for" Nera Brahmashiva turned to leave, "Nera Parvati and Nera Kashyap, please join me in my quarters" He said over his back.

====XXX===============

"What do you think, why has he summoned us?" Nera Kashyap as he tried to keep pace with Nera Parvati as they walked down the long corridors of Gurukule.

Nera Parvati with her wild auburn hair and piercing eyes, was one of the sharpest minds especially went it came to mental warfare. Nera Kashyap, the younger and sturdier, bore a rugged charm. His caramel-colored hair and a well-groomed moustache felt like an extension of his nose. His thick, bushy eyebrows nearly shielded his dark eyes. To the ignorant, he would appear more like a groomed caveman, particularly definitive due to his stocky built than the scholar he really was. Although a lot younger than most of the Neras around, Nera Kashyap's accomplishments surpassed his age. In fact, it was his uncanny knowledge and exemplary strategic skills that earned him a permanent place in the closest circle of Nera Brahmashiva's top aides.

"The death of Nera Hung, must have something more than what he had just discussed" Nera Parvati said casually. She was busy adjusting her long white robe, whose ends were roughly brushing against her ankles.

"Come in Neras" Nera Brahmashiva answered to Nera Kashyap's soft knock.

The grand yet humble office of the Nera supremo was a place of great of contrasts. Carved out of pure oak, it had two parallel libraries on either side. One half stacked with ancient manuscripts, while the remaining half was left strikingly modern with hardbound books, of every possible genre. It was in between these two libraries, where the small seating arrangement could be found. Comprising majorly of a huge LCD monitor on the left, a large wooden desk in the center, and a few fur chairs placed in a circular file, the seating was way too humble for a man of Nera Brahmashiva's stature. But this wasn't where Nera Brahmashiva was usually found. Whenever restless, he preferred standing by the large French window at the western corner of his office. The giant icy valleys underneath seem to provide him the direction he sought.

"What troubles you?" Nera Kashyap finally broke the silence, "Isn't everything unfolding as foretold?"

"It is", Nera Brahmashiva paused, "but Nera Hung's curse has revealed secret about Tvashtar's end". His brows frowned, "If Tvashtar deciphers the curse, he will be forewarned. And as we all know, he will stop at nothing to find the boy".

"Then why not bring the boy here, within the security of Gurukule?"

"It is not time yet. Besides, he is too young to understand his powers." Nera Brahmashiva dismissed the idea with a gentle wave of his hand, "the boy must come to understand the weight of his destiny. We are not allowed to make choices for him, our reasoning can only guide". He leaned back stiffly on the large fur chair behind the round wooden desk.

"But he is our only hope. At the very least, we should keep an watchful eye on him" Nera Parvati insisted.

"The problem is", Nera Kashyap made no attempt to hide his frustration. "We still don't know which one is *him*"

"Yes, that's exactly why I had called you two" Nera Brahmashiva stared deeply at his closest allies. "Neras, this is utmost confidential. From now on, I want both of you to be always around these boys, but be very careful not to reveal your identities. Tvashtar and his men are surely looking for this boy and I cannot risk them recognizing either of you."

The man outside Nera Brahmashiva's office smiled faintly, his hand absently adjusting his odd-looking horn-rimmed glasses perched on his nose.

===============================XXXXXXXXXXXXXXXXXXX===========================

Far, far away from Gurukule, another figure moved swiftly through the night. His long jet black hair streamed behind him like of whiff of wind, his muscles bulging through the contours of his black shirt, his half-Hispanic-half-Indian face taut.

His emerald-green eyes gleamed in the dark- sharp and alert. His long-pierced ears twitching. He had been running for months, years now, chasing whispers and tales, piecing together fragments of legend.. His job was to hunt down that "someone", so that his King could live. This man was called Ankara, and he was a Tracker.

Anvantaras had always been cautious. From their earliest days, they had trained their youth to become Trackers. A Tracker was an Anvantara who had undergone rigorous training to sharpen all the five senses to the absolute peak. Their mission was to hunt down any threat to the Anvantaras. Among them, Ankara was perhaps the finest Tracker of his generation. So when Tvashtar issued the order to find that "someone", Ankara was the natural choice for the task.

Ankara had traversed nearly every corner of the world- except northern most parts of India. Over the years, he had encountered countless tales, but none had ever been worthy of his pursuit. Now, as he darted through the dense woods near this small village nestled in the shadows of Himalayas, he couldn't help but ponder the curse. Was it truly real? What would his King think if he returned empty-handed, without finding "the one". Lost in his thoughts, Ankara moved swiftly through the woods, rarely pausing for anything. Narrowing his focus, he pressed his long fingers against his temple, trying to concentrate on what had sensed.

"Hey Himanshu, wait up!", a small boy shouted, his voice echoing through the quiet evening air.

Himanshu turned, irritation flickering in his voice, "What? It is getting dark Chandan".

"Just hold on! I got something to show you" Chandan said excitedly, "You remember that story Papa told you about Arjun?"

"About Arjun?"

"Yeah, the boy who killed a giant crocodile with his bare hands when he was just eight" Chandan barely able to contain his excitement

"Not that ridiculous village tale again!" Himanshu groaned.

"No, it is true!" Chandan insisted. "ask my Papa- he was there when it happened"

"But why is it important now?" Himanshu growled, his tone impatient.

"You see that house up there" Chandan pointed towards the shadowy mansion on the hills, its silhouette looming against fiery colors of the setting sun.

Himanshu nodded slowly.

"Arjun used to live there." His voice dropping to a whisper, as if the house itself could hear them.

"Where is he now then, can we meet him?" Himanshu asked with a half-mocking tone, more to test Chandan than out of any genuine interest.

Chandan sighed "No, he has gone for higher studies."

Ankara raced through the woods furiously, trying to reach the boys on time. But by the time he arrived, the boys were long gone.

Standing there, Ankara stared at the mansion bathing in twilight, "An eight year old boy, who can kill a crocodile, is certainly worthy of my attention. I have to find you, Arjun"

===============================XXXXXXXXXXXXXXXXXXX===========================

If somebody saw them for the first time, they might mistake them as siblings. The resemblance was uncanny- same striking brown hair, deep blue eyes, and a refined aura. The only difference were their builds- Jignesh was tall and athletic, while Vibha was slender and delicate.

"I still don't see why we haven't moved to Mumbai yet?" Vibha snapped, her frustration evident. "How do you even know our little boy is doing fine without us?"

She missed her children, but Jignesh, due to reasons best known to him had turned a deaf ear to her for all these years.

"He is not a little boy anymore, he is thirteen now" Jignesh reminded coldly. He hated these never-ending discussions, which kept surfacing every second day. "Kavya, Jenny and Gene, Parth, and Sara, all are there, why do you need to be there at all?"

Jignesh sighed loudly, his patience thinning. "He is not a little boy anymore. He is eleven" He loathed these recurring arguments. "Kavya, Gita, Lena, Parth, Sara- they are all there. Why do we need to there as well?"

In recent years, the Anands had made strides up the social ladder. With Avneesh Anand now managing Jignesh's entire wood business, his status and influence had grown significantly. So it came as no surprise when Avneesh Anand along with the Mehtas, decided to send all his four children to Mumbai for higher studies. The arrangement was a win-win situation for both families. The Mehtas were pleased that the three Anand sisters, were there to look after Arjun and Sara. Meanwhile, the Anands reveled in pride of a historical milestone- for the first time in countless generations, their children were leaving the village for higher studies.

Vibha turned to retort, but was interrupted by a loud knock at the door. It echoed through the nearly empty mansion, stark against the Dussera's quiet night. Grumbling, Jignesh rose to answer the door.

"Yes?" Jignesh asked the stranger.

With his suave looks, the man outside appeared fairly well groomed and harmless, "E-e-evening Sirrrr," the man stammered, his teeth chattering in the biting cold. Jignesh couldn't take his eyes off the man's long, expensive looking cloak flapping violently in the wind, "my name is Rehan Ankara, I am a tourist, Sir. Actually, my car broke down. Could you please direct me to the nearest garage?"

Jignesh sighed, his breath forming a frosty cloud between them "The nearest garage is eight miles from here. But come in, it's freezing outside" Jignesh Mehta invited Ankara in, oblivious to danger lurking beneath his polite demeanor. Perhaps it was his lingering quarrel with Vibha, or maybe his sheer benevolence, but Jignesh failed to notice the absence of the night watchman. Had he peered into the shadows, he might have seen the lifeless body of the watchman slumped behind the trees.

"This is my wife" Jignesh introduced Vibha, gestured towards her with a strained smile. She stood, her posture rigid. She wasn't pleased. She just gave a brief nod. "Mrs. Mehta, could you make us some coffee; this gentleman seems cold and tired". He looked at her pleadingly, "May be you should stay here tonight, I don't think anything can be arranged before the morning" he told Ankara.

Vibha gave her husband a long, stern look, before resentfully retreating to the kitchen. She was visibly upset. She wondered if her husband had invited a stranger to stay to deliberately avoid her.

"Forgive my wife; she is a bit upset with me" Jignesh said with an awkward laugh.

"Sir, you forgive me for intruding on your evening" Ankara replied, his voice smooth.

"Not at all. I am Jignesh Mehta" Jignesh smiled as Vibha returned with the two mugs of steaming coffee; she had over boiled the milk, her frustration manifesting in the bitter brew. Her hands tightly held the tray, as she placed the mugs sharply on the table, as if hoping the hot brew would burn them both.

"Ma'am" Ankara stood, offering her his seat. But Vibha shook her head and sat as far as possible from Jignesh; the silent war between them was far from over!

"It's just two of you in this big house?" Ankara glanced around their grand living room, lingering on the family photos on the wall above the fireplace.

Vibha nodded curtly.

"No children?"

"No" Her voice, clipped.

"Oh, I am so sorry" Ankara said, feigning sympathy

"Actually, we have a son," Jignesh interjected with an uneasy smile. "He is in the city". He pointed to one of the many photographs adorning the walls. The one Jignesh pointed to was from his eighth birthday. Arjun was wearing a dark maroon suit, something he had found girly and embarrassing, however Vibha thoughtlooked adorable; Arjun on the other hand, loathed it, he didn't even smile for the picture!

"What does he do in the city?" Ankara tried to keep his tone casual.

"Arjun is in school" Vibha said, her face softening for the first time that evening. She missed her son terribly!

"Interesting name, Arjun" Ankara remarked. His eyes gleaming with a strange intensity. "Which city did you say he was in?"

"Mumbai" Jignesh readily replied, unaware they had just walked into a trap.

Ankara's demeanor's shifted abruptly. He stood, his movement deliberate. "Mr. Mehta, I think I should leave"

"Now?" Jignesh asked, surprise spanning across his face.

Ankara nodded, a sinister smile playing on his lips as he tossed aside his cloak, "I must return to Mumbai, there is this boy, I need to take care of"

Vibha looked at her husband, puzzled, but Jignesh needn't no explanation. The protective father lunged at Ankara but the stranger was faster. With a swift shove, Jignesh crashed into a chair, splintering it beneath his weight.

"What is happening?" Vibha whispered weakly, her eyes widening with horror. Her heart hammered as Ankara swiftly tied them both to the sofa

"Because your son.... is a threat to my King" Ankara replied coldly.

"But we don't even know your King. And Arjun is just a boy, there must be some mistake" She pleaded, her mind racing. How could her boy, be a threat to anyone, let alone some King.

"No mistake" Ankara said, his voice icy, "Your son is a Anvantara."

Jignesh's eyes burnt with fury, "If you touch my boy, I will kill you"

Ankara smirked, his voice controlled. "Don't force me to hurt you, Mr. Mehta. You have been a gracious host" He turned to leave but paused, his hand resting on handle of the door, "On second thought, why take a chance?" He stepped back in, closing the door with a final, ominous click.

===============================xxxxxxxxxxxxxxxxxxx============================

"What a mess this rain has made" He muttered, striking a match to light a pipe. The flame flickered briefly before settling. Outside, the downpour showed no signs of settling, its steady drumming on the windows rattled the silence within his throne room.

In the depths of a realm where light had long since abandoned hope, Tvashtar sat upon a throne fashioned from the bones of fallen Anvantaras. The Throne Room of the world's most powerful King was testament to his grandeur, befitting to a ruler of his stature. Spanning the size of a football field, it was colored in pearl blue, his favorite hue. But, despite its vastness, the walls remained strikingly bare, save for one the behind Tvashtar, which proudly displayed an imposing portrait of the sovereign himself. The only other adornments were the two parallel rows of opulent navy blue chairs, meticulously arranged on either side of the majestic golden throne, which rested upon an elevated platform at the heart of the chamber.

"We have news, His Highness", General Kofi Raj announced, his voice echoing in the vast hall.

"Good or bad?" Tvashtar almost looked straight through the General, as if he was just an apparition.

"His Highness, both actually" The General replied cautiously.

"Tell me" Tvashtar shifted uneasily on his throne. Restlessness clung to him like a shadow, it had been three years since his men commenced searching for the young Anvantara, and still, no success. The relentless rain only amplified his agony.

"Our Tracker believes he has found a boy" The General said, "One who maybe the Anvantara born amongst humans"

Tvashtar leaned forward on his throne, his eyes narrowing. "Tell me more"

"The boy is rumored to have killed a crocodile with bare hands when he was just eight or nine years old"

Tvashtar shot to his feet, his voice laced with pride and urgency alike, "Only a true Anvantara can do that; haven't you heard, a fully grown Anvantara alone can take down a whale if not a dinosaur." His excitement flickered, "But are we certain he is the 'one'?" He paused, his voice softening as though speaking to himself, "But even if we are not, he is dangerous. Kill him. We can't afford to take chances".

"The Tracker is already onto it, His Highness" The General assured him.

"I hope your Tracker does the job well" Tvashtar's gaze darkened. "I am not used to disappointed, Kofi Raj"

"Ye...Yea... His Highness" The General stammered, unnerved. It was rare, unsettling to be honest to hear their King use first names.

"Anything else, General?" Tvashtar aimlessly lingered on to his pipe for a while, not smoking, simply fiddling with its circular end.

"Yes, His Highness. Boris Bladis has been elected the President of Russia. We now have the East Europe under our toes, but..."

"But?" Tvashtar's stared up sharply.

"Britain and the US are being resilient. We have failed to sway their leaders with either wealth or intimidation"

A slow, mysterious smile panned on his face, as he reached out for the intercom beside him, "Send in Doctor Nowell"

The General's face contorted. "Doctor Nowell, His Highness?" His surprise was evident. Doctor Mukund Nowell, the head of Tvashtar's elite Science Team, reported directly to Tvashtar. His line of work was shrouded in mystery, even from Tvashtar's inner circle. If rumors were to be believed he and his Science Team were building biological weaponry, but no one knew the full extent of Doctor Nowell's work.

Tvashtar walked over, adjusting his General's dark green necktie beneath the Army tunic, with an unsettling intimacy. "What money and fear cannot do, science can" Tvashtar whispered. The General stood frozen, scarely daring to even breathe with his King so near.

"But his methods are unorthodox... sometimes, even fatal", the General muttered, stepping away slightly. It wasn't just Doctor Nowell's methods that unsettled him; it was the man's blatant disregard for the General's authority as the head of Tvashtar's massive army.

"Doctor Hudson Nowell." The heavy doors creaked open as concierge echoed through the hall.

The ginger haired Anvantara scientist stepped inside. His lean frame moved with an odd, swaying rhythm, his bony, long hands swinging slightly by his side. A white lab coat was carelessly thrown over his ill-fitting formals and the black wayfarer glasses completed his thoroughly indifferent appearance.

"Afternoon, My Lord" he bowed. |Then shot a dry, indifferent smile towards the General "General". The disdain between them was mutual, "You summoned me, My Lord?"

"What's been the progress, Doctor?" Tvashtar asked as he walked back to his throne.

"Oh!" Doctor Nowell flinched, as if the question annoyed him. "It's been proceeding well. The weapon should be ready by early next year." The scientist's accent was oddly slurry.

General Kofi Raj shifted uncomfortably; it was rare for him to be kept in the dark and his King's secrecy stung more than he cared to admit. He would have preferred to dismissed outright, rather than left standing there, with such apparent lack of information.

"I will visit your lab soon, Doctor" Tvashtar declared

"We look forward to it, My Lord" Doctor Nowell replied, bowing once more before exiting the room.

As the doors closed behind him, General Kofi Raj's curiosity gnawed at him, but he hesitated to speak.

Tvashtar looked at him and chuckled. "You want to know about the project, don't you?"

"W-W-Well, no, Your Highness, I can understand if you want to keep it confidential" General Kofi Raj cursed himself for fumbling once again.

"How long have I known you General?" Tvashtar asked. His tone light yet dark.

"Close to a hundred years now, Your Highness"

"And you feel I don't understand you, General?"

"No, No, Your Highness, that's certainly not what I meant" The General stammered yet again. It clearly wasn't his day.

Tvashtar's smile returned, cold and assured. "General, all I can tell you is this: Doctor Nowell's team is crafting something so lethal, that once complete, it would establish supremacy of the Anvantaras- forever!"

IV
Mumbai

He glared at the empty tube of hair gel in his hand, its contents now smeared meticulously through his hair. Staring into the mirror, he barely recognized the twelve-year-old boy staring at him. The dark haired, skinny kid from Nagvari was long gone. In his place, stood someone broader with a more defined- though somewhat round face. His once wild, curly strands were now tamed into a fashionable side part. *If only, I could lose that double chin*, he thought, tilting head to assess his jawline.

"Jenny, it's just a dinner", he barked, pounding on the bathroom door.

"Two minutes, Parth", came his sister's muffled reply.

Before he could retort, Gene, his seventeen-year-old sister walked in, her fingers fiddling with hem of her oversized turquoise top, which hung loosely over her ripped, denim shorts. At five feet three, she was chubby and hazel eyed like her brother, but slightly darker. "By the way where are we going?"

"McDonalds" Parth announced flatly.

"Where's Kavya?" Jenny stormed out of the bathroom, her white cardigan flaring over a pink tank-top, and matching skirt. Jenny was a leaner lookalike of Gene "Where's everyone, Parth? Why is it only me you rush?" She huffed, her hands on her hips.

"Oh Mademoiselle, everyone else is ready" Parth sneered, "We are just waiting for you"

The orange, old, rickety Suzuki hatchback wheezed like it was on its last breath, parked precariously along the narrow lane by their small apartment. Over time, it looked less like a car, more like a jigsaw puzzle of discarded pieces slapped together in a hurry.

Kavya had been honking incessantly since she arrived. The eldest of siblings it seemed had lowest patience. She was clearly mad at them, but that didn't stop her from stealing glances in the rearview mirror. The baggy, red shirt over the long gray skirt was left unbuttoned near the neck; the thick, brown bead necklace matched against her deliberately ruffled brown hair—giving her the perfect hippie look that she yearned for. But, unlike her sisters, Kavya was slimmer, taller and undeniably prettier. It was almost strange how little she resembled the rest of them.

"If you guys are not coming, I will go and grab Arjun and Sara myself!" Kavya turned the ignition as they climbed in.

"Parth's girlfriend is joining us too?" Jenny teased at the mention of Arjun' cousin.

Kavya grinned into the mirror. Parth couldn't help blushing. He liked Sara; but having his sisters talk about her was torture! "Eyes on the road, grandma!!" The girls giggled at their brother's frantic attempt to deflect the topic.

"Kavya right, take the right from the signal," Gene shouted as the jalopy turned a corner, "It's a short cut to Link Road"

Gene was right, in less than twenty minutes, they rolled up in front of the McDonalds at Borivali West. Arjun and Sara were already there, waiting.

Arjun looked the same- his athletic frame solid, his dark brown eyes sharp beneath the messy mop of long hair. His hands rested protectively over Sara's, her delicate fingers a sharp contrast against his. Sara looked petite in her short yellow frock, her eyes sparkling beneath long lashes.

"Hey" Parth greeted, his voice softer than he intended.

"Why so late?" Sara casted a playful glance at her watch, "we thought you guys had cancelled the plan. Arjun was about to call"

"Ask the ladies, I was ready in no time" Parth shot back.

"Yeah, the minute he heard that you were coming" Jenny chimed in, earning a murderous glare from her brother- one that faded the moment he saw noticed Sara blushing too.

"Man, let's eat" Arjun groaned, uninterested in the teasing; his focus was singular: food.

The McDonalds outlet was mostly empty- a few couples tucked here and there, a loud Gujarati family taking half the dining area.

"The menu seems so much better than the bland rice thali at school" Sara exclaimed, thumping her table loud enough to turn heads. Embarrassed, she ducked behind the menu card.

"If we are done with the drama, can we order now?" Arjun snarled, his patience wearing off.

The food arrived quickly and seeing them pounce over it like some hungry puppies, even the McDonalds' staff couldn't resist their smiles. But the children didn't care, they were simply too busy savoring the contents on their plate, so busy in fact, that no one noticed when Kavya quietly slipped away.

But when she returned, things had changed dramatically.

Her face was completely drained of color; "Guys, we need to leave...Right now!" Her voice was barely above a whisper yet sharply authoritative. That was the first time that they even realized that she had stepped away.

Jenny licked the mayonnaise off her fingers, "What's wrong, Kavya?"

Kavya didn't respond. Her jaw hardened; eyes fixed ahead. That alone was enough. They knew her well enough to sense something was seriously wrong. One by one, they gathered their things and followed her out without another word.

Back in the car, the tension was thick. But, Arjun never one for silence, snapped. "What's going on Kavya?" He grabbed her arm, forcing her to meet his gaze.

But Kavya could not. "Arjun, your parents have met with an accident" Her voice wavered.

"Where they are now? Are we heading back to the Nagvari?" Sara asked worriedly.

Kavya's face stiffened. "No"

The single word sent a chill through them

"Then?"

Kavya swallowed hard. "The Mehta' mansion caught fire, and...." There was a strange guilt, remorse in her eyes. She took her time to choose the right words, "...they were caught inside"

Her phone buzzed and she quickly walked away again, murmuring into the handset. "No, I wouldn't leave them" she whispered into her phone. The others stood frozen, the weight of her words settling over them like a dark cloud.

Parth couldn't take it anymore. He approached her quietly. But Kavya hung up at his very sight.

That's when he heard it – just five words whispered in a rush before the line went dead *"The Tracker Ankara killed them!!"*

V

General Thoris

"Who is Ankara?" Parth' question was too direct.

Kavya shot her brother an uncomfortable glance, "Let's go" she murmured, deliberately avoiding her question.

"B-But" Parth lingered, his curiosity gnawing at him. He couldn't figure what secret his eldest sister was guarding so fiercely.

"Why are we not going to Nagvari?" Sara interrupted. Her eyes were still red, fresh track of dried tears marking her face.

Kavya took a deep breath. "You girls will be going back to the Nagvari"

"And what about us?" Parth asked, his voice laced with confusion.

"We got somewhere else to be." Kavya's words were clipped, hurried. "Girls, I am dropping you home. You all are big girls now, I am sure you can take care of yourselves. My Papa will drive you three to Nagvari tomorrow morning"

Kavya didn't even care for their replies as she stepped on the hatchback's accelerator.

===============================XXXXXXXXXXXXXXXXXX===========================

Over an hour later, before Kavya finally pulled up in front of the busy Terminal 3 of Mumbai Airport.

"Where are we going?" Parth's voice was tinged in disbelief, as they joined a long queue outside of many gates to the imposing two-storey building.

"Srinagar"

"Srinagar, Kashmir?" exclaimed Arjun in a very controlled surprise. Showing a trace of emotion after the stoic silence all this while.

Kavya met their stares laced with uncertainties with steady eyes. "I know you have questions but trust me, you will get your answers. Just... not now... please don't ask"

"Tickets and IDs?" The lean looking security guard interrupted them.

"Anita, Anuj, and Anish Agrawal" Kavya rummaged through the purse for the National IDs. The man scanned their documents and allowed them to step inside the airport. Parth & Arjun exchanged glances. Kavya had lied boldly-without flinching!

===============================XXXXXXXXXXXXXXXXXX===========================

Kavya placed a tray of sandwiches and cola on the empty chair between the boys "Eat, you must be hungry".

The boys, still grappling with the whirlwind of events, reluctantly picked at the food. Their unfinished meal at McDonalds seemed like a distant memory.

Arjun finally broke the silence, his voice low but steady. "Tell me something Kavya, were my parents murdered?"

Kavya's eyes softening. She nodded softly. Parth stared at her in disbelief.

Arjun's stoic façade wavered. A lump formed in his throat, the weight of unspoken grief pressed down upon him. He had feared this truth ever since that caveman had first warned his father about it. His father had prepared for many things, but not for pain of the reality. Yet, Arjun had a promise to keep- the pride of the illustrious Mehta family could never be compromised. That meant no tears, neither in silence nor in solitude; he had to be that rock that seeps in everything without any qualms and complaints, and emotionlessly it stays a rock, forever.

A crackling announcement interrupted his thoughts "May I have your attention please. Flight Number 6E686 is ready for departure. Passengers please proceed to gate number 43B for boarding".

The anxious boys followed Kavya through the glass doors. Beyond gate number 43B, massive planes stood like silent sentinels, their lights flickering in the dark, moonless night.

==============================XXXXXXXXXXXXXXXXXXX==========================

The grey sky over Nagvari was cloaked in grief. It was a day of mourning, a village united in sorrow to pay their last respects to two of their most cherished souls!

"How did this happen??" an old lady whispered, her voice trembling.

"I wish I knew" replied a plump, middle-aged lady, "I wish I was there to help".

But not all hearts were weighed down by grief. A lone figure stood at the edge of the crowd, silently observing the service from afar. He hadn't left for Mumbai that night, knowing the city would be too big, too crowded, too risky for his plans. But here in the quiet of the village, all he had to do was to find the bereaved boy alone.

Nagvari was in full attendance at the funeral. One by one, they all kept arriving, everyone but Arjun.

His heart missed a beat when Jignesh's green sedan slowly pulled up next to the crematorium. So, this was it, his three years' quest was now about to conclude.

Dressed in a white shirt, Avneesh Anand was the first one to step out. Gene, Jenny, and Sara, all dressed up in white dresses silently followed him, but that was it! No one else came out of the car! No little boy, no Arjun!

Arjun' sudden absence from his parents' funeral hadn't baffled Ankara alone, even the villagers seemed stunned over the unprecedented turn of events. But, before the murmurs could catch up, Avneesh signaled the priest to commence the rituals.

Ankara stood fuming; his misery knew no bounds. Where was Arjun? What was more important than attending his parents' funeral? His mind buzzed with questions. None of which he could answer. But, one thought loomed larger than the rest, *'What would he tell Tvashtar?'*

==============================XXXXXXXXXXXXXXXXXXX==========================

General Kofi Raj had been twitchy today; pacing the throne room nervously. Ankara stood silently, his lips pursed and his eyes lowered, unwilling to meet anyone's gaze.

"What do we have here?" The doors swung open and Tvashtar entered the Throne room.

"His Highness, there is something you have to know"

"Spare me the nonsense, General" Tvashtar snapped, "Was he the *'One'*?"

"We believe so"

Tvashtar's piercing gaze settled on Ankara, "Then I reckon the man standing behind you is legendary Tracker Ankara?"

Ankara dropped to his knees at once. His long, black military jacket almost crumpling under his heavy weight, but the usually well-dressed Tracker didn't really care; Tvashtar's temper was well-known, "Your Highness, please forgive me"

Tvashtar waved dismissively, "Tell me about this boy Tracker"

General Kofi Raj sighed; relieved to be out of the firing line.

"H-His name is Arjun," Still on his knees, Ankara began shakily, "H-His Highness. Born in Nagvari..." He looked up at his King, for the first time since he had arrived in the throne room.

"I am listening" Tvashtar growled. He studied Ankara intently; there was something unnervingly familiar about him, a flicker of recognition tugged at the edges of his mind. Yet, despite the nagging sense of déjà vu, Tvashtar was certain that they had never crossed paths in person.

Ankara recounted every detail, sparing nothing. He needed Tvashtar to understand- it wasn't incompetence, it was sheer ill-luck.

Tvashtar's eyes gleamed coldly. "Then he is the *'one'*!!!!"

Ankara nodded, hopeful.

"You know Tracker" Tvashtar continued, his voice cold, "One thing my father always said...." Ankara kept dipping with each word his King spoke, as if trying to show his utmost loyalty, his undefeatable respect for the crown, "...being defeated and being dead are the same things" Tvashtar bent slightly and rested his hands over Ankara's strong shoulders, gesturing him to stand. Ankara nodded weakly, the gesture meant hope, he thought. But mercy was not in Tvashtar's nature!!

General Kofi Raj shivered in anticipation; Ankara was a very valuable asset, the best indeed. But then, Tvashtar never forgave people who lost, not in his ranks, at least.

"Someone clean-up this mess" Tvashtar said casually, wiping his hands with a blood-stained handkerchief. Ankara was lying in a pool of blood, his head ripped off, and his body still convulsing.

General Kofi Raj felt sick but stunned. Sick at the treatment his Tracker had just received, but stunned to see how effortlessly Tvashtar decimated such a power-packed Anvantara. The *Pud* had indeed enhanced Tvashtar's powers beyond imagination.

"Care for a drink, General?"

"Your Highness" General Kofi Raj fought hard to find his voice. He had always known of King Tvashtar's brutalities, but witnessing it first hand- against one of their very own- was a chilling reminder of Tvashtar's ruthless reign

==============================XXXXXXXXXXXXXXXXXX=========================

Parth squinted against the bright sunlight as they stepped out of the plane "Where now?"

The weather was unusually pleasant for May, a fact that only struck Parth later when he realized they were in Kashmir, where it was always cold. But, Kavya was oblivious to the crisp air; she was busy texting on her mobile.

"Where to?" A scrawny looking man popped out of a white cab as they exited the airport.

"Waligi" Kavya said without looking. Her fingers were still busy typing on her mobile.

The man sounded surprised. "That's three hundred kilometers!"

Kavya finally looked up, her eyes sharp and unwavering. "Want to go or not?" She asked curtly.

The man hesitated, then grumbled "Okay, but it will be very expensive" He stepped out to open the door, "These rich chics and their royal plans" He muttered under his breath.

Kavya heard him but didn't react. She simply motioned the boys to get in.

As they slid into the back seat, Parth shifted uncomfortably on the brown leather seats, they smelt stuffy. "Why are we going to Walgeri?"

"Waligi" Kavya corrected, her tone clipped.

"Yeah, why are we going to this place?" Parth was getting jittery. He had almost traveled half away around the country, yet answers remained elusive.

Kavya gave him a stern, unyielding look, and it was getting too familiar now! Every question he asked seemed to meet that same impenetrable wall "Let's discuss when we are alone?"

As the cab rumbled out of Srinagar, the bustling cityscape gradually gave way to serene countryside. Rolling hills blanketed in lush green stretched out before them, the sweet scent of fresh air seeping through the windows. It reminded the boys of Nagvari—beautiful and uncomplicated. But, the peace outside did little to calm the storm of questions swirling inside Parth's mind.

==============================XXXXXXXXXXXXXXXXXX=========================

Nestled on a meadow atop the mountains, Waligi actually exuded the grandeur of a royal retreat. A dozen opulent country houses dotted the landscape, their elegance stark against the eerie silence that enveloped the place. Not a bird fluttered on their roofs, nor a soul peeped out from the windows. The houses stood frozen in time, their stillness sharply contrasting with the noisy, little stream that found its way behind them, its water sparkling like diamonds under the dusky sunlight.

"Over here Nera Kavya" A red skinned, pot-bellied old man in a yellow baseball cap and a loose sky blue shirt waved at them from a distance. He stood beside a sleek, silver prototype of the plane that had delivered them at the Srinagar Airport.

==============================XXXXXXXXXXXXXXXXXX=================

"Who else is here?" Tvashtar asked, swirling the scotch in his glass, the amber liquid catching the dim light of the throne room.

"Your Highness, as much as I hate to admit" General Kofi Raj began, avoiding eye contact, his own glass untouched "Ankara deserved a second chance"

"Who else is there?" Tvashtar repeated, disinterestedly.

"A few, but none match Ankara's skills"

"You know General," Tvashtar mused, his fingers tracing the condensation on his glass, "There was a man once- General Thoris. Do you remember him?" he looked at his General, his fingers still fiddling with ice cubes in his glass, "If this boy is what we believe him to be, we cannot afford loose ends. We need our best to hunt him down".

"General Reoah Thoris?" General Kofi Raj stiffened. It was a miracle that he hadn't exclaimed, "He would never work for us, not after what you did to Ankara"

Tvashtar looked at his General quizzically.

"General Thoris is Ankara's brother, Your Highness"

"Thoris is Ankara's brother?" Tvashtar's eyes widened as if a puzzle piece had finally clicked into place. "That's why the Tracker looked so familiar! All this while, I wondered where I had seen him before. Now I know- he is General Thoris' brother"

"And Your Highness, General Thoris now lives is retired" The General added, cautiously.

"Truth, General is often a matter of presentation" Tvashtar said, draining his scotch, and setting it down with a decisive thud, "Send for Thoris. Tomorrow morning!"

===============================XXXXXXXXXXXXXXXXXXX==================

The man who entered was unmistakably Ankara's kin- short, silver hair and aging features aside, he bore the same narrow eyes, long pierced ears and hooked nose. His dark blue suit clung to his muscular frame, a testament to his enduring strength, even in retirement.

"Long time, General Thoris" Tvashtar greeted with a thin smile, as Thoris offered a crisp salute.

"Your Highness, I was told you wished to see me" Thoris said, his tone clipped and professional.

"I have a task for you, General" Tvashtar began cautiously, his voice soft and deliberate.

"I believe you have the wrong man, Your Highness. I am retired".

"I am aware of that General"

"Then why summon me?"

"You know General, my father once said a just King should never deny an avenger their vengeance"

"I am afraid I don't follow, Your Highness"

"My dear General, be brave when I tell you this" Tvashtar walked down the aisle towards Thoris, but for some reason paused midway.

"Is everything alright, Your Highness?"

Tvashtar had a grave expression on his face. "General, your brother Colonel Ankara was a man of unparalleled bravery. I was told he fought valiantly until his last breath." Tvashtar watched Thoris intently. The words struck Thoris like a thunderbolt. His face paled, his eyes hollowed, and his knees buckled. General Kofi Raj rushed to steady him, guiding him to the nearest chair.

Tvashtar watched them from afar, "How Highness, how?"

"The details are unclear" Tvashtar said, his voice laced with a convincing mix of sorrow and sincerity, "but I was informed he was killed by an Anvantara boy called Arjun in a village near the Himalayas."

"What do you want me to do?" Thoris' voice trembled, yet his Anvantara DNA kept him from crumbling.

"General, I want you to avenge your brother. Find this boy and kill him"

"But Your Highness, why me? Surely there are others more suited for this task"

"Because you are the brother, Ankara loved and revered. The honor of avenging his death belongs to you and you alone" Tvashtar walked further down the aisle this time, his face still sounding sincere "General, I am a just man, that's why I want you to avenge your brother's death, but if you feel you no longer have the strength, I can understand. It's been years since you last wielded a weapon" his tone carried a subtle sting, "Perhaps, I should assign someone else. I cannot let Ankara's sacrifice be in vain. Never" He paused, letting the weight of his words sink in before delivering the final blow. "You know what pains me the most, General?" Tvasthtar's eyes locked into Thoris's, "This boy, Arjun desecrated Ankara's body, and fed it to animals. Barbaric Savages!"

Thoris's eyes blazed with fury, his grief metamorphosing into a seething rage "I will hunt down that boy, Your Highness. No matter the cost, he will pay with his life, you have my word." His voice was low growl, thick with rage.

Tvashtar exchanged a satisfied glance with General Kofi Raj as they watched Thoris march out of the Throne Room, his fists clenched but his shoulders hung low; the old general had clearly been dented.

"Your Highness, are you sure Thoris is the right choice?"

"I couldn't think of anyone better".

"But, he is retired!"

"General, let's hope he is at least half as ruthless as he once was, and our boy, Arjun will be pleading for mercy."

==============================XXXXXXXXXXXXXXXXXX=======================

Bahadur sprung to his feet. The old warrior gait was heavy, his shoulders slumped under an invisible weight.

"Master, what happened?" He couldn't hide his concern. Of Nepali origin, Bahadur had a rather humble career as an orderly in Thoris' office, but even after his retirement, he had remained by his side, as a devoted loyalist.

Thoris didn't reply, he walked past Bahadur and collapsed onto worn cane chair; his face sinking into his trembling hands, "Bahadur" the mighty Thoris sobbed, "We have lost Ankara!!!"

Bahadur stiffened. In all these years, he had never seen his master like this! He wanted to ask hundreds of questions, yet he refrained. Now was not the time.

Swallowing hard, he slowly walked up to Thoris, "Master... I don't know what to say. Master Ankara was a great man" But the words felt inadequate, but Bahadur had nothing more reassuring to say, especially when he had no idea what had befallen Ankara.

Thoris didn't budge, didn't blink. "I will hunt him down Bahadur. I will hunt the boy who killed Ankara. I will find him, and make him pay" He looked hard at Bahadur.

"But Master" Bahadur hesitated. He didn't have any doubts about Thoris's abilities, but the very thought of Thoris rekindling his brutalities of his past made Bahadur shudder.

"No-ooo...Bahadur" Thoris pushed him away, "Call Ali and tell him I need two drunk elephants at his school. I start training tomorrow."

Professor Ali Beg, the Dean of the Anvantara Institute, a very prestigious training school for Anvantaras Trackers, was a Thoris' childhood friend.

Bahadur's eyes widened in horror.

==============================XXXXXXXXXXXXXXXXXX=========================

Kavya looked surprised. "Didn't expect to see you here Nera Barney" She confessed.

The plump, affable man grinned. He looked like a man with no burdens, no past "Only a fool would miss this summer, Nera Kavya"

Parth found it odd- the way they addressed each other as 'Neras' as if it was some sort of a title.

Nera Barney's eyes drifted to the two boys standing behind Kavya. His eyebrows shot up in an exaggerated surprise. "Oh my God, is one of these really the Mighty Vyom Vardhan?" Nera Barney gasped softly.

Parth and Arjun exchanged confused glances. They had no idea who or what was Mighty Vyom Vardhan was. Their expressions too left little to imagination.

Nera Barney chuckled but didn't push further "Let's go boys"

It was for the first time, the boys had seen a cockpit up close. The panel appeared like a complex switchboard, way too many dials and levers to memorize. The loud roar of the engines soon gave way to a smooth whoosh, as they could feel the gravity beneath them.

"You guys hungry?" Nera Barney yelled over the noise of the airplane, and he certainly didn't care for an answer, "There's food in the freezer behind, go help yourself. Come on now, don't be shy"

The hour passed quickly. At quarter to seven, Nera Barney finally turned to them, "We land in another half hour...Gear up boys"

Parth peered out of the window, expecting to see city lights below. Instead, there was only darkness. He cupped his hands around the glass, peering harder. All he could make out was a thick blanket of swirling black clouds , floating like puffs of smoke.

"Where are we?" He asked at last

"We are approximately five-fifty miles from Neranche" Nera Barney replied, pulling out white fur coats, ice glares, and a bunch of white-colored woolen caps from the compartment behind the cockpit. Each item 'Gurukule' embroidered in bold red letters.

"What's Neranche?" Arjun asked. The name sounded exotic.

Nera Barney looked disbelievingly at Kavya. "You didn't tell them about Neranche?" Then he turned back to them, "Boys, Neranche is a city located in central Kailas"

"Kailas? We are in Lord Shiva's Kailas?" Arjun's jaw dropped.

It was impossible to grasp. In less than thirty minutes, they would be stepping into a land they had only heard of in stories.

===============================XXXXXXXXXXXXXXXXXXX========================

Minus the incredible purple sky, the one of most mysterious places on earth was little more than an endless stretch of white wilderness, a barren desert of snow. And if that was not enough, the sky itself had transformed dramatically. The warm, welcoming purple hue they admired just minutes ago had deepened into an ominous black, and the notorious Himalayan winds have begun to howl mercilessly. But, even in such inhospitable conditions, Nera Barney seemed at complete ease.

In fact, the boys didn't even realize the flawless transformation of Nera Barney from the pilot to an enthusiastic tour guide, leading them southwards across the snow-covered plains toward a long, man-made ice tunnel.

The mile-long tunnel ended abruptly at the base of a colossal hill- one of the largest the boys had ever seen. Nera Barney, who was still chatting to Kavya, let his hands expertly work on some random combinations of rocks on the hill

And then suddenly, massive hill began to split apart, its icy walls groaning as they parted like two halves of an enormous door.

Beyond it, concealed from the outside world, lay a vast and magnificent hidden city!

VI

The Gurukule

For anyone raised in the twenty first century, Neranche felt like a city straight out of fantasy. The boys would have pinched themselves when Kavya waived down a dark brown wooden carriage pulled by two milky white horses.

"Where to, Madam?" The elderly chauffer inquired.

"Gurukule" Kavya replied with a usual familiarity as she helped the boys climb the carriage. The carriage smoothly glided through the broad concrete streets, flanked on both sides by towering pine trees. It appeared as if they had been planted intentionally forming a natural barrier that concealed the sprawling houses behind them. Built from light brown bricks, these homes were undeniably impressive, yet their true distinction in spite of their sizes lay in their symmetry- so perfectly aligned that none appeared grander or humbler than rest. But despite the sheer scale of the city's architecture, the sight of horse driven carriages and citizen draped in cloaks and medieval styled loose shirts and pants created an almost surreal contrast. It was as if time had come to a standstill in Neranche's pursuit of modernity.

Their awe however was short-lived. The carriage suddenly veered onto a narrow, uphill path, where deep, icy valleys below looked treacherously steep. Even those few pine trees here and there, appeared only as glorified defenses against dreadful mishaps that seemed inevitable. Just as the last of the pine trees vanished, a dark, imposing structure emerged at the far end of the road.

It was difficult to say what lay beyond those towering walls, but as the carriage halted in front of a massive copper gate, the boys took in the intricate emblem running along its entire length- a pair of entangled golden lions. Above the gate, inscribed in metallic copper letters was the name of the institution: **GURUKULE CENTER FOR ADVANCED ANVANTARA LEARNING**

"Nera Kavya," A towering guard, easily over eight and a half feet in silver armor, greeted Kavya with a stoic nod before pulling a lever to slide the gate open.

===============================XXXXXXXXXXXXXXXXXXXX=========================

Everything about Gurukule oozed a wow.

A long pathway- built partly on ground and partly suspended in air, connected them to a rock platform that housed all the buildings afar. Torn picturesquely between the icy Himalayan ranges and the immense dark lake, a set of five buildings haughtily stood atop a colossal rock platform. The platform itself was precariously perched on a massive fifty-foot boulder, so seemingly delicate in its balance that boys hardly dared to breathe. Each of the five structures was an architectural marvel, uniquely embodying the four cardinal directions. The east wing resembled a monastery, the west wing was a sleek blue glass edifice akin to a corporate office. The north wing took the shape of a fierce ice castle complete with a huge dome on the top, while the south wing appeared like a deep cave amid a dense jungle. Yet, among all these impressive buildings, it was the Central Office gleaming entirely in gold!

"I will take your leave now, Nera Kavya. And yes, before I forget, Nera Brahmashiva is expecting you guys" Nera Barney excused himself, leaving them beneath the grand facade of the Central Office.

Kavya was back in charge.

Confidently, she led them through a labyrinth of long, confusing, castle-like corridors. The long, deserted corridors were adorned with countless paintings and mantelpieces, each piece of art wrestling for space between heavy, polished, wooden doors.

"Come in", a deep voice resonated as Kavya knocked on one of the wooden doors.

Kavya pushed the door open to reveal a grand sandalwood-scented office.

"Good evening...Nera Brahmashiva Sir" Nera Kavya folding her hands respectfully.

The man facing them was striking- tall, an easy air of wisdom and long braided silver hair. His short, silver-grey beard was trimmed neatly above his slightly pouted neck. Like the archaic dressed people at Neranche, he too wore a thick, straight collared, white, fur cloak over the starched white robe hanging over his broad, gaunt shoulders.

"At last, I see them" Nera Brahmashiva spoke, his voice so clear and calm that it sounded almost like the purest form of sound, "I wonder which one of them is *him*, though I wonder how little they both look like Vyom Vardhan". He held Parth by his face, his long white fingers holding his face so serenely that Parth didn't even feel his touch; though the gesture left Parth wondering why him? Why only Parth was being studied?

"Vyom Vardhan?" Parth found himself ask. This was the second time Parth had heard the name, first from Nera Barney and now Nera Brahmashiva.

Nera Brahmashiva smiled, "I know your questions boys. But before I answer them how about a cup of hot chocolate?" His own eyes twinkled at the thought, "Sit down. You have come a very long way."

Kavya stifled a smile; she knew how much Nera Brahmashiva relished hot chocolate. Nera Brahmashiva rang the small golden bell on his table, and an elderly man four steaming cups.

Nera Brahmashiva took a sip, his voice steady yet serious, "Boys, there is a reason you are here"

"Because you guys think that whoever killed my parents would now be after me" Arjun interrupted, unwilling to relive that agony all over again

Nera Brahmashiva nodded understandingly, "Son, you must understand- those responsible aren't ordinary people. They are very powerful"

"But I have never harmed anyone. Why would they want to hurt me?"

"Because your fate is your foremost foe"

"My fate is my what, Sir?"

The Nera Supremo smiled as he set his cup down, "Let me tell you a story, boys. Around two million years ago the evolution of human beings began. They evolved from monkeys to apes and eventually to humans. And that's when their evolution process stopped. But little did they know that there was one race of humans, for whom, the evolution process hadn't stopped. These beings continued to evolve into super intelligent, and super powerful human beings known as Anvantaras. The Anvantaras had been living amongst humans ever since their evolution, and have been commendably successful in camouflaging their identities. Though sometimes, when required, they had to reveal themselves, but their tales always got lost as mythologies; Jesus, Odin, Zeus, Rama, Cupid, Shiva, they were no mythological characters, but Anvantaras, who had let their larger than life image effect the humans in away that made them appear as Gods. That's how the Anvantara race had so successfully concealed their identities."

Parth's mind reeled. "But how does this involve us?" Parth asked.

Nera Brahmashiva's eyes held their gaze "Because you are a Anvantaras, both of you. And not just any Anvatara, rather very rare ones!"

The revelation felt too unreal to be true. Parth half expected to wake up from a dream. But the Nera Supremo's unwavering conviction left no room for disbelief.

"A very rare Anvantara?" Arjun asked cautiously.

"Yes, one of you may even be a reincarnation of the Mighty Vyom Vardhan".

"Reincarnation?" Parth had no clue what the word meant or for that matter who this Mighty Vyom Vardhan was, but the word "mighty" was good enough to hold his interest

"Reincarnation means rebirth" Kavya clarified.

"Then Arjun is your man" Parth cleared, much to the discomfort of his best friend, who shot him an uncomfortable glance, "I can't be some reincarnation. In fact, I have never done anything mighty or heroic, Arjun has." Parth continued uninterrupted, "He had killed a crocodile with bare hands" he was now not even looking at Arjun, "Even my parents are just ordinary humans."

"That's the beauty of it" Nera Brahmashiva chuckled, amused by the remark. "Once or at the most twice in ten thousand years, an Anvantara is born to human parents".

"Who was the last person before us then, the Mighty Vyom Vardhan?" Arjun asked, his voice had a subtle hint of sarcasm. They had heard the name Vyom Vardhan far too many times.

Nera Brahmashiva smiled softly. "No, it was the king of India, Rama and his younger brother Laxman. Just like you, they too had human parents"

"Let's say even if we believe you, how is it possible scientifically?" Parth challenged; the Nera Supremo's stories defied all logic!

"Good question!" Nera Brahmashiva mused, glancing at the last remnants of the hot chocolate in his cup before shifting his focus back at them, "For such a phenomenon to happen, at least one of your parent's ancestors must have been an Anvantara. Typically, Anvantaras marry within their own race, for obvious reasons. But love, as you know, follows no rules. Many Anvantaras have found love outside their race, some even marrying the humans or had children with them" Nera Brahmashiva paused, finishing the last few drops of what remained in his cup, "However, for a child to be born as an Anvantara, both parents have to be Anvantaras, just one Anvantara bloodline alone isn't enough. That said, children born to human-Anvantar unions still inherit Anvantara genes, even if they are dormant. And, when two such humans with Anvantara lineages or dormant genes, come together in a holy union, there is a one in a million possibility that their dormant Anvantaras genes would fuse to give birth to a true Anvantara, even if both parents are human"

Parth was the first one to speak. "Well, first of all, I don't know if I am an Anvantara. I have no powers like Arjun" Parth stated "And even if I am, surely I am not the only one born to humans in past thousand years, right?"

Nera Brahmashiva nodded

"I mean, Arjun too had human parents, and he is very powerful" Parth clarified, nonetheless.

Nera Brahmashiva's steadied his tone, "Yes, like you, Arjun' parents had Anvantara lineage; Vibha didn't know about that fact as both her parents had passed away when she was a child. But Jignesh knew and chose to not discuss it with his wife. But, on Arjun' fifth birthday, we sent one of our Neras to enlighten Jignesh and Arjun, just as I am doing it now"

Parth turned to Arjun, startled. Arjun, however, remained impassive. Parth looked back at the Nera Supremo. "Even if I accept everything you said...How can you be so sure that one of us is the reincarnation of this Varun guy"

"Vyom" Nera Brahmashiva corrected, "Because we follow stars. Every individual on this earth has star assigned to them. When a person dies, its star fades away, only to reappear when their soul is reborn. The 'al-athanan' also known as the Golden Knight Star was seen shining above both of you at birth. It was the same star that once shone over Vyom" Nera Brahmashiva took a deep breath, "Do you have any idea how long we have waited for that star again to return?" his voice, usually steady and calm, turned a little hoarse, revealing just how much Vyom Vardhan had meant to him, "I know, the truth is sometimes hard to accept, but the truth is not always what we see"

"But why now. Why weren't we brought here before?" Parth still wasn't convinced.

"That's because your enemies didn't know where you were, not until now"

"But who are these enemies? We have never harmed anyone, and I am as powerless as it gets. Maybe Arjun is in danger"

Kavya gulped, "Even your enemies see Arjun as a threat. But, since the *al-athanan* was seen over both of you, we couldn't afford any chances."

"Then how will we ever know which one of us is the true reincarnation of this Mighty Vyom Vardhan?" Parth asked; if they kept guessing, they would never get an definite answer.

"Only the true reincarnation of Vyom Vardhan can command all the five elements of this universe- Air, Water, Earth, Sky, and Fire" A voice announced.

Kavya stood up immediately, "Evening Nera Parvati Ma'am, evening Nera Kashyap"

Nera Kashyap and Nera Parvati nodded as they stepped into Nera Brahmashiva's office. Parth suddenly realized that Nera Parvati was the same woman he had seen sitting right behind Kavya on their flight from Mumbai. Had she been following them all along?

Dressed in flowing white robes, she looked different from the woman in violet slacks and black top, he had earlier seen. Parth noted that except for Nera Barney, all the senior figures at Gurukule wore similar white robes- perhaps a uniform or a dress code.

"I can't believe I am seeing them again" Nera Kashyap confessed in a controlled tone.

"Sir, just one last question" Parth interrupted, his eyes still set on Nera Brahmashiva, "Is Kavya also one of you? I mean one of us? An Anvantara?" It dawned upon him that Kavya was the one who had brought them to Gurukule.

Nera Brahmashiva nodded.

"Which means even she was born to human parents too?" Parth asked hesitantly.

"Not really" Nera Brahmashiva sighed, "Nera Kavya isn't your biological sister. Some twenty years ago, a little girl was adopted by your parents, unaware that we had facilitated that adoption, although it was eventually informed to your parents."

"But why?"

"So that she could be with you boys, till you came to Gurukule"

"And what is that you expect us to do at Gurukule?" Arjun asked.

"Study and train till you are ready for the challenges ahead"

"And what if I refuse? What if I say that I just don't belong here? What if I just want to go back to my home?" Arjun' emotions were dribbling.

"Then we wouldn't stop you" Arjun looked at Nera Supremo, surprised. Nera Brahmashiva would give up that easily? It was hard to believe "Boys, you must understand that we brought you here, that too now, only for your safety. But, Gurukule is no prison, it is just another educational institution and we are its facilitators, if you may call us so. We can equip you with necessary skills needed to face greater challenges, but we cannot make decisions on your behalf. Your battles will always be yours to fight"

Nera Brahmashiva patiently waited for an answer;

Parth sighed, he didn't know how else he should react. Part of him still questioned everything, yet another part was thrilled by the new revelation- like a superhero in making. Even Arjun, usually unfazed, gave a nearly invisible nod.

"Huraka, please take the boys to their room" Nera Brahmashiva called out.

The same old man who brought them hot chocolate stormed back into the room "Masters ... follow moi tu ure ryoom" He instructed in a thick local accent.

=============================XXXXXXXXXXXXXXXXXX=========================

The Anvantara Institute buzzed with excitement. It wasn't every day that someone trained with the wild elephants.

"Professor, General Thoris has arrived" An attendant informed the bespectacled old man. Prof. Ali Beg had the face of a philosopher, who had never quite found acceptance in the society, yet that never deterred him from trying. His hands were unusually short for his height, but they were elegant, like an artist, clean and pure. Carefully, he straightened his now crumpled black suit, ran a quick hand through whatever remained of his white hair and a matching French beard.

Thoris didn't bother to knock, but then Prof. Ali Beg never minded when his oldest friend walked in unannounced- besides his visits were rare.

"How are you old man?" Prof. Ali Beg greeted him with a warm smile. It had been years since they had last met, yet unlike him, Thoris hadn't slouched an inch. Prof. Ali Beg observed this with mild envy.

"Not well, Al" Thoris didn't attempt to mask his pain.

"So I heard" Prof. Ali Beg replied, recalling his conversation with Bahadur, "But whatever is destined to happen will happen Thoris, we rarely have any control over the fate" He said, although he was not sure how much comfort it provided.

"Al, you did you get me the elephants I asked for?" Thoris asked, disinterestedly.

Prof. Ali Beg nodded "I did. But are you sure about this? You have aged, Bud"

The Centrimica was massive- larger than any football field, with a seating capacity of over fifty thousand. It was grander than what Thoris had expected for a mere training ground.

"Built recently?" Thoris noted.

Prof. Ali Beg smiled.

As the two men entered the amphitheater, it erupted with applause.

"I thought I was training alone" Thoris's said, narrowing his eyes.

"My friend, with the elephants arriving, the news spread like wildfire" Prof. Ali Beg sighed.

Thoris frowned, "I hope you at least made sure the elephants were adequately boozed up, right?"

Prof. Ali Beg nodded.

"Then let them out, Al".

The crowd roared as two massive African elephants stomped into the field, their brown hides gleaming under the lights. Their small eyes and large floppy ears acknowledged the audience, their trunks swaying over formidable pale tusks. But something was off- someone had miscalculated the dosage. Instead of aggression, the beasts wobbled unsteadily, their movements clumsy yet strangely graceful to the oblivious spectators. This was bad news for Thoris.

The apparent lack of interest from the elephants had started to annoy Thoris. Irritated, he picked up a big rock and hurled it at one of the elephants. The elephant bellowed in pain, and locked eyes with its assailant- Thoris now had its complete attention.

The charge of an elephant is a breathtaking spectacle- if you are not the one being charged at. It is rare fusion of ferocity and elegance, the ground trembling under their weight. And, with Thoris more than willing to reciprocate the animal's attack, the crowd held its breath in anticipation of a unique contest.

First, came the vicious trunk swipe, Thoris leapt to his right, but years of neglecting his training showed. He landed hard, panting, rolling away from the beast. Prof. Ali Beg had been right, his friend had aged!

The apparent lack of practice came at a heavy price.

In his pursuit of the first elephant, he had completely ignored the second. A sudden brutal impact sent his world spinning- the second elephant's trunk slammed into him like a battering ram. Thoris flew across the field, crashing straight into the southern gate. The crowd gasped.

Prof. Ali Beg rushed to the fence, "You okay, Bud?"

Blood dripped from the general's elbows, his breaths ragged. Seeing the struggle, Prof. Ali Beg immediately signaled for the guards to contain the elephants, buying Thoris few precious moments to recover.

But Thoris wasn't done. His eyes locked onto the larger of the two beasts, he rose slowly, steadied himself, and sprinted forward. Gripping its trunk, Thoris hauled himself onto its back; Timing his moment, he prepared to strike the beast's head- bring it down. Then he could deal with the second one.

But, the elephant was faster than he had expected.

With a sudden swung of its trunk, it grabbed Thoris in a crushing grip and flung him into the iron fences. The impact was even more brutal- his head hit the ground first while his body rammed against the steel fences, moments later. Thoris slumped, motionless, his once white shirt now streaked with the red and brown.

Prof. Ali Beg knew this was it; he had to call more guards, medics- whatever it took to contain the elephants, and salvage what remained of his aging friend.

But, before even he could act, the elephants wailed outrageously and charged back. Stopping just inches from Thoris, both elephants gradually raised their massive front legs.

The stadium trembled with cries of terror. Some in audience watched, spellbound, others squeezed their eyes shut, bracing for the inevitable.

And then it happened.

His hands shot up, catching the weight of each charging elephant. His muscles strained under their weight; his veins throbbed madly beneath his mud-streaked shirt. For a moment, he stood motionless, locked in sheer defiance of nature itself; his eyes staring into the horizon. Then with a power beyond fathom, he flung the elephants across the fields into the fences, which crumbled under their weight.

The amphitheater burst into unanimous applause.

But Thoris wasn't done yet.

One by one, he dragged the elephants back to the center. Gripping their trunks, he started swinging them in the air as though the elephants had suddenly turned weightless. And when he finally released them, their mutilated bodies crashed into the farthest corners of the field.

Brutality has always been his biggest strength and today Thoris reminded the world of it.

The amphitheater rose to their feet in awe and admiration, the *'Brutal'* Thoris was back!

===============================xxxxxxxxxxxxxxxxxx========================

Two towering giant men, sculpted from polished white marble, stood with their hands joined, forming the grand entrance to white Monastery of the East. Their tall, curved, luminous bodies radiated an ethereal glow. The East Wing's interiors echoed the elegance of its exterior- pastel, pristine and timeless. But it was the strange tranquility of the place that truly captured Parth, momentarily making him forget the countless questions swirling in his head.

"Dis iz colled Shaantilok, d eazt wing, et bruings peayce n oenergy. Nera Brahmashiva say dis is ver ure stor zyuper iz nyow, in d eazte" The old man from Nera Brahmashiva's office broke the trance.

Parth turned towards the man, sensing that probably he might be the only person who could finally answers the questions both Kavya and Nera Brahmashiva had so cleverly evaded. "Sir, tell me something, how well did you know the Mighty Vyom Vardhan?" The old man's quick steps came to an abrupt halt. He didn't reply, instead signaled at the pale wooden door, one of the many in the long row of small rooms that lined the right side of corridor.

For some reasons Parth was certain that this old man held the key to the secret of Vyom Vardhan- the figure of legend, the one reincarnation had shaken the very foundations of their world. What was he like? How did he look like? Was he truly like one of them? The revelation had left Parth with a million unanswered questions.

"I knew Vyom" He spoke at last. "Ofcourz he wos nyot the Mighty Vyom Vardhan thenn, but eh veory broight, soft spouken buoy I must sayee. Some-wone hu wos vyery grunded evon ofter knowing tat he huld so myuch powor, only if he hudn't follen for datt ogli trick"

Arjun's ears perked up "What ugly trick?" The old man stiffened. He had spoken too much.

"Nouthing Master Arjun, I must leove nowe. U twu get syome sleep" without another word, he left.

Parth sighed and turned the brass handle to their new home in Shaantilok.

The place was simple- white plastered walls, two single beds, a wooden cupboard, a couple of study tables, and a large window that overlooked the breathtaking icy valleys below. Arjun immediately claimed the bed facing the window.

To their surprise, the wooden cupboard was already stocked with fresh sets of clothing. The top two racks held neatly folded white and dark blue shirts, steel grey and white pants, couple of steel grey sweaters and two black fur cloaks. Below, four pairs of white socks, two pairs of black shoes, and two steel grey ties bore the insignia of Gurukule. The last rack had a pair of white towels rested beneath a blue envelope- The school was structured into four academic levels: Junior Grade (Classes 1-10), Higher Secondary Grade (Classes 11 & 12), Graduate, and Postgraduate levels- The boys joined in class 7 of Junior grade. Inside the envelope, they also found the hostel instructions, route maps and class schedules.

A soft knock interrupted their exploration- Krenz had returned balancing a large tray of food. He set it down gently on one of the study tables, leaving the boys to their well-earned feast. Tired from the long day, they hit the beds with vengeance.

But for Parth, the rest was fleeting.

His first night at Gurukule was no different; The same nightmare clawed its way into his sleep,- the masked horseman was back.

He woke up drenched in sweat.

Half past nine.

Damn! He had overslept.

Frantically, he shook Arjun, but his friend barely even stirred. With no time to waste, Parth grabbed a towel and followed directions from the blue envelope, to find his way to the washrooms. Parth noticed that even corridor had enough signages- washrooms, cafeteria, gymnasium, and the recreation center. Slowly, he walked down the sunlit corridors towards the washrooms, reading the directions, and memorizing them for future.

The hostel washroom was simple- rows of white sinks on one side and short wooden doors for blended chores- shower and ablutions on the other. He took his time to adjust the temperature on the shower. The warm water felt good against his tired skin.

Until-

"Sorry" He muttered absentmindedly; stepping out and accidentally bumping into someone.

A sneering voice cut through the air. "You little rat" Someone screamed.

Parth snapped up. A towering boy in his late teens glared at him. The muscles on his body, he just wasn't any student.

"Sorry," Parth repeated wearily, "I didn't see you"

The boys lips twisted into a smirk "Freshman"

In a flash, he yanked the white towel off Parth's chubby waist.

A wave of dread washed over him. The last thing he wanted was to commence his time at Gurukule by picking a fight- especially with someone twice his size.

"Return my towel" Parth demanded, his voice steady

"Oh I will" The boy said mockingly. "But first, let me throw you a welcome party, bud. You don't want me to be a party pooper, do you?," A few more of the boys joined the bullying senior. "So, if you are willing run around this corridor twice, naked, then I might consider returning your towel" The smirk not leaving his face.

"Return his towel" Arjun stood at the entrance; his eyes dark "Now"

"Or what, you little prick?" The gathered crowd of students erupted into laughter.

Arjun didn't hesitate. "I was only thinking about complaining to Nera Brahmashiva, but now that you have given me the idea..." he struck first, a sharp kick to the gut. The boy sat down, writhing in pain.

"How dare you hit Bob?" A tall boy with African features lunged forward in retaliation, but Arjun was faster. Sliding on his hips, he rammed into the boy's legs. The senior crashed into a sink, shattering it into pieces.

==============================XXXXXXXXXXXXXXXXXXXX==========================

By the time the boys returned to their room, Parth was still processing what had just happened. He glanced at the instruction manual still lying on his bed. With a sigh, he flipped through it's

pages. Parth discovered that every Gurukule student had to take at least five subjects in their first year - three theoretical papers and two outdoors. After a moment's thought, he settled on basics of survival strategy, modern warfare, and Anvantara history as his theory papers, and fencing and arm combat as his outdoor subjects. It wasn't passion that drove his choices- only necessity. The subjects felt as unfamiliar as the school itself.

Arjun, ever indifferent, didn't even glance at the manual; he just dittoed Parth' subjects.

Their first class was scheduled at half past eleven.

Although the white shirt, the steel grey pants and the sweater fitted him fine, yet it was the tie that bothered Parth. No school he had ever attended required a tie. And back home, his father always fixed it for him! After several failed attempts, he wearily shoved it into his pocket.

"Where to Lad?" Parth heard a crisp British accent. An old, bald man in the customary white robes of Gurukule. Heavy freckles dotted his kind looking face.

"Modern Warfare class, Sir"

The man pointed down the corridor "Third door on the right". The Nera smiled, "But I think your class has already commenced. Better hurry up, Nera Reran isn't exactly popular for his benevolence" He patted Parth on the back, gesturing him to hurry. Parth nodded in gratitude, hurrying towards the classroom.

But as soon as he stepped inside, he was met with a dozen pairs of curious eyes staring at him.

A short, dark-haired man in a ruffled white robe frowned. "Who are you?" He had a typical nasal tone.

"Parth" he replied as politely as possible, "I am in your class, Sir"

Nera Reran adjusted his thick glasses, "Oh! Then I'd would say, you are very early... for the tomorrow's class" His tone dripping with sarcasm.

Laughter erupted.

Parth stomach sank. "But Sir, I am only five minutes late!" Parth had clearly missed the sarcasm.

More laughter.

Heat rushed to his face as he backed out of the classroom, praying no one had seen his humiliation. But the corridor was packed. And Nera Reran's voice wasn't exactly subtle.

He walked back to his room as fast as his legs would allow when a voice stopped him

"You are Parth, right?"

A boy his age grinned at him, his long dark curls bouncing as he spoke. His easy confidence was disarming.

"Hi, I am Santosh, Santosh Jacobs. I am in your modern warfare class." Santosh extended his hand with an affable easiness.

He shook it, confused, "How do you know me?"

"How do I know you?" Santosh seemed amused, "Man, your friend Arjun is already famous. After what he did to the seniors this morning. Everyone knows you both now"

Parth didn't reply; unwilling to relive the morning's events, "If you are in my class, then, why aren't you inside Nera Reran's class right now?"

Santosh grinned, stretching lazily "Well, thanks to you. I was right behind when you were facing the music".

"So you were late too?"

"Overslept" Santosh stifled a yawn.

===============================XXXXXXXXXXXXXXXXXX=========================

"So, Parth finally has his first friend at Gurukule" Nera Parvati remarked, "Bright chap, this Viswanathan fellow. At least we can be sure the boys will survive the academics"

"Is he related to Colonel Shriram Viswanathan? Kavya asked, glancing at her.

"Santosh is his son" Colonel Shriram Viswanathan was a reputed Nera Commander, and the security-in-charge of Gurukule.

Meanwhile, outside her office, a bespectacled man stood, looking perplexed. He couldn't understand why everyone at Gurukule seemed so concerned about these boys, who were they? He knew one of them was Nera Kavya's brother, but being Nera Kavya's sibling alone wasn't enough to command attention of the top Neras!!! He needed to gather more facts- there were significant perks to sharing the right information with the right people!

===============================XXXXXXXXXXXXXXXXXX=========================

The sun finally felt soft and cool, casting a pleasant glow over the bustling city. Even the usual rush seemed overrated today. His heart pounded with exhilaration, his lips itching to shoutin triumph. Who would have thought he was still capable of this- even after hundred twenty years of retirement? It felt good to be back, to be alive!

The lanky young man in a plaid suit dialed a number on his mobile, "Sir, the subject has regained his powers." He reported, speaking quickly. "Yes it was good; very good... Yes, I am on his trail"

Thoris was still in a daze as he parked his car, walked into his study, and switched on his silver MacBook. The screen flashed the top results for NAGVARI.

Bahadur peered into the computer screen, "Aren't this boy's current whereabouts still unknown?"

"Honestly Bahadur, I don't know" Thoris confessed, fingers entwined on the table. He had no plan- yet, "May be I should start from Nagvari, where he was last seen"

"There is way, Master, I don't know what it is called, but it originated in our country in the early fourth century." Bahadur said, pulling a chair beside him "A Tracker seeks help from the animals and birds to locate its subject, but I doubt anyone remembers how to do it now"

Thoris stared at Bahadur for a long moment. Then suddenly thumped his fist on the table "You right, you are so damn right." His excitement was spilling from each word. "But of course, why didn't I think of this before? What better way to find this boy than Faunatics"

"Faunatics?" He repeated, puzzled.

"That art is called Faunatics Bahadur, that lost art is called Faunatics".

"But it's a lost art, Master"

"Indeed it is" A strange sparkle appeared his eyes, "Don't forget I am old school. From a time where everything wasn't about technological aids" His voice brimmed with enthusiasm of a school boy, "If everything else is coming back, then so will this. And when it does, there would be no stopping!" His finger hit "confirm flight" button hard.

==============================XXXXXXXXXXXXXXXXXX=========================

In the humungous cafeteria, Santosh slurped his porridge nosily "What subjects do you have?" With over an hour before the Modern Warfare class, they had enough time for breakfast.

Parth buttered his toast thoughtfully, "Let's see... There is Modern Warfare, Basics of Survival Strategy, Anvantara History and for outdoor subjects, I believe I opted for Fencing and Arm Combat."

"And Arjun'?" Santosh asked, his curiosity never-ending.

"The same as me"

"Hmm" Santhosh gulped down a spoon of porridge, "So, we will be together for three classes" He poured himself some orange juice, "Except I have Economic Techniques instead of Anvantara History, and Mixed martial arts instead of fencing." He licked a stray drop of juice off his index finger "But more or less you are in safe hands"

Parth looked up, puzzled.

"You see, History is taught by Nera Norton- one of the many lost souls wandering around" Santosh explained, "And fencing by Nera Nehatara, she may seem a bit jittery at first but trust me, she has her own set of priorities- which clearly figure above her classes"

Parth listened intently. He needed this kind of information to survive at Gurukule. But did he *want* to survive here? That was the real question.

"So where is Arjun?" Santosh asked.

It was getting annoying. He couldn't go a minute without bringing up Arjun. Parth could only wonder how Santosh would react if he ever found out that Arjun was a rumored to be the reincarnation of the Mighty Vyom Vardhan.

"He is joining the Survival Strategy class directly. He was late for the first one, so he skipped it altogether". Parth sighed. He wished he had done the same- it would have spared him the public humiliation.

"Tell me something" Santosh lowered his voice.

Parth braced himself, not another question about Arjun, please. "What?"

"Where is Arjun from?"

"Nagvari. A small village about hundred miles north of Simla. We are both from there" But Santosh barely acknowledged Parth's origin. His interest was fixed on Arjun.

Santosh looked startled. "Simla in Himachal Pradesh?"

"Yes, why?"

"Nothing, it's just that we've heard rumors about a young, super powerful Anvantara- unknown and unseen- who would descent from great heights to save our world" Santosh said, voice dramatic, as if narrating some historic Hollywood epic.

Parth narrowed his yes, ""And?" He wondered what is coming next, *'I heard that this boy is the reincarnation of the Mighty Vyom Vardhan?'*

"And, I thought may be Arjun is that Anvantara." He admitted sheepishly. "I mean, how often do you see a young Anvantara take on a bigger Anvantara, and beating him hands down?"

Parth stifled a smile, "You may be right! May be Arjun is that unknown and unseen Anvantara". He liked the words- "unknown" and "unseen". He decided to play along. "Besides, Nagvari is approximately four thousand feet above sea level. That technically makes Arjun a returnee from the great heights, assuming you consider four thousand feet as a great height"

"I don't really know" Santosh sighed, sincere in his confusion. "Nobody ever quantified the height. But I always imagined it has to be the Himalayas"

Parth bit his tongue to keep from laughing. "How would I know?"

Santosh helped himself to another bowl of porridge, meanwhile Parth waited for his second helping of toast,

"So, when did you guys arrive at Gurukule?" Santosh seemed busy processing the information.

"Yesterday, Nera Brahmashiva wanted us to join"

Santhosh almost choked on his porridge. "Did you say that Nera Brahmashiva personally asked you to join Gurukule?"

Parth rolled his eye. "Cut the theatrics, Santosh"

"Who are you man? Who are your parents? I mean-" He shook his head in disbelief, "Oh, why am I even asking? Your parents must be some super big shot Anvantara, right?"

"Not really"

"Don't bluff, Nera Brahmashiva rarely meets students- especially first year, junior grade. Are you kidding me?"

"Trust me Santosh, my parents are no big shot Anvantara. But my sister Kavya is a Nera at Gurukule" Parth deliberately dropped her name, hoping to learn more about her

"Kavya, um…" Santosh expression shifted, "Kavya. You mean Nera Kavya? The one who teaches advanced weaponry?" Parth nodded, even though he had no clue what she taught. "Dude, she is a super-hotshot Nera- one of Nera Brahmashiva's top aides." Santosh exhaled, as if everything finally made sense. "Hmmm, that explains why he met you in person"

Parth seized the chance to change the topic "Why are all Professors called Neras here?"

Santosh gave him a long, condescending look- one that suggested that Parth had just asked what color the sky is.

===============================XXXXXXXXXXXXXXXXXX=========================

They had no idea what the word strategy meant when they first stepped into their survival strategy class. But, strategy wasn't the only thing that they were clueless about. Lifelong backbenchers, the boys had never considered the pros of sitting in the first row. In fact, Parth often wondered why anyone would voluntarily place themselves under the watchful eyes of their professors. But when Santosh took a seat on the first row, Parth had no choice, but too follow. Arjun though reluctant, joined them.

Nera Michelle, the Basics of Survival Strategy professor, was a middle-aged woman with an impeccable sense of style. Her neatly trimmed auburn hair barely grazed the golden colored collar of her crisp white robe. "Afternoon Class" She greeted them in a husky voice.

"Good afternoon! Nera Michelle" the entire class responded in unison.

"So, is everyone ready with their last week's assignment "How to survive if caught in a tornado'?"

This time, only a few students answered. Parth glanced around nervously. To his horror, Santosh was first to raise his hand. One by one, each student stepped forward to submit their assignment, while Nera Michelle strolled through the class, scanning the faces around her. Parth's anxiety grew as Nera Michelle neared them, Arjun however sat unperturbed. His stoicism continued to shock Parth.

"You're new?" She stopped at their desk.

"Yes Ma'am, my name is Parth"

"Ah right" She tried to hide the excitement in her voice, but her eyes gave her away, "Nera Brahmashiva mentioned you too- new students joining mid-term. One of you is Parth, and the other is… Anuj. No Arjun, correct"

"That would be me" Arjun replied just as the bell rang.

But their academic struggle just didn't end with the Survival Strategy. If anything, it intensified as they navigated from one unfamiliar subject after another.

Nera Rudolf Norton was the epitome of a History Professor. With long, unruly white hair, thick, unkempt beard, and a tattered white robe stitched together in too many places to count, he looked as prehistoric as the subject, he taught.

"Turn to chapter 17, the era of Reno, The King of Thymus" He mumbled in a barely audible voice.

The boys quickly realized that passing Nera Norton's subject required not only sitting in the front row- his voice barely reached beyond the second row- but also memorizing the same dates for both BCs and ADs!

===============================XXXXXXXXXXXXXXXXXX=========================

As Thoris stepped out of the New Delhi Airport, he turned to a security guard. "Where can I hire a car?"

"Walk straight, take the first left. Last shop on your right, Sir"

The bright blue neon sign against yellow background assured him he was in the right place,

"How may I help you Sir?" A young man behind the counter asked.

"I need a car from New Delhi to Nagvari"

The man looked up, confused. "Nagvari?" He clearly hadn't heard of the place.

"It's a village about a hundred miles north of Simla" Thoris scoffed, irritated by the man's lack of knowledge about his own country.

"Simla" The man smiled sheepishly, "Any preferences?"

"Any sturdy SUV"

The man took his time searching through the system. Impatient, Thoris tapped his foot against the floor "No problem, Sir. We have a Toyota Innova available. May I see your driving license and passport?"

================================xxxxxxxxxxxxxxxxxx=========================

The morning was so cold, even the sun seemed reluctant to rise. Out of the two boys, Arjun was usually the lazier one, yet when Parth woke up that day, Arjun was already gone.

They had two classes scheduled - Arm Combat at ten, followed by fencing, at three in the afternoon.

Parth searched the room for their route map, but it was nowhere to be found. Arjun must have taken it with him. With no choice, Parth set off alone, navigating the enormous Central Office on his own. Finding his way through the vast corridors was as daunting than as facing Nera Reran in his worst moods.

A sudden flutter of wings startled him. Alone in a dimly lit hallway, he realized he had taken a wrong turn. Instinctively, he picked up pace- only to trip over something and go tumbling down a rough sloping path. He landed in what looked like an operating theatre. A thin, pale man in a lab coat, stood at the table dissecting a dead bird with a large blue beak and orange round head.

"Who are you?" The man grumbled in a voice so deep it seemed to rise from the depths of his empty bowels.

"P-Parth" He stammered as he pushed himself up.

The man's unblinking stare made Parth uneasy. "Parth, I see. A probable reincarnation of Vyom Vardhan" The man muttered, roughly grabbing Parth's chin with his blood- stained hand, "So what do you want from me?"

"Nothing, I just got lost" Parth took a step back.

"What's the hurry Parth?" He laughed, setting aside a heavy, freshly sharpened knife "Don't you enjoy my company?" He slithered even closer.

"Sir, I have a class. May I leave?" Parth's pulse quickened.

Before the man could respond; the bird let out a shriek and in an instant, the knife came down on its head. That was all the permission Parth needed- he bolted, running as fast as legs could carry him. He only stopped when he reached a group of students gathered outside a small stadium.

Santosh and Arjun rushed over "Where had you been?" Santosh asked.

"Lost" Parth was panting badly.

"What's that on your chin? You hurt?" Arjun wiped away the dried blood as Parth recounted what had happened.

"Must be Nera Shiraj," Santosh mused. "He teaches Para-Biology to graduates. We call him the 'Spooky Shiraj'. He is always this scary and mysterious!"

"The Arms Combat class is starting" A short, stout boy with Japanese features called out. His short brown hair was styled into a Mohawk.

Zonre 1, as the training ground was called, was a small enclosure with a central stage and about fifty seats arranged around it.

"I hate this class" Santosh complained in a low voice, "If my dad hadn't forced me..."

The mention of his father made Parth realize how little they knew about Santosh, "Why, what's wrong?"

"This is where Nera Vesper gets to bully us- officially" Santosh pointed at the well-built man with slicked black hair, standing on the stage.

"But who can bully a Anvantara?" Arjun asked, surprised.

"Everyone! In case, you haven't noticed we are all Anvantaras here" Santosh grumbled.

"I wonder who today's victim will be" A girl behind them whispered.

"No, don't look up… look down, look down" someone else murmured.

"Shall we begin?" Nera Vesper's gaze swept the class, almost everyone kept their head down- except Arjun who was a second too late, "Yes you, the new boy. What's your name?"

"A-A-Arjun Sir", he fumbled. The students had already done their part to dissuade the newcomer.

Nera Vesper gave him a long, appraising look "Come up" A relieved faces in the crowd exhaled. "See, since you have volunteered…" he smiled. "We'll do a demonstration, Vyo, err Arjun, right? A hesitant Arjun nodded. "Watch carefully, then we'll see if you can replicate it"

A rather tall guy named Doug stepped forward. The two men bowed slightly before taking their positions like seasoned wrestlers analyzing each other. Doug had the advantage of his size, but the students soon understood why Nera Vesper was the Professor. With a sudden yank, he slammed his chest against Doug's, and delivered a powerful kick that sent him reeling.

"You see how it's done?" He grinned at Arjun's petrified face, "Now, your turn now"

Arjun barely had time to react before Nera Vesper locked Arjun's hands into his, and that was the last thing Arjun remembered before he found himself smashed against the wall. Blood trickled down his forehead as he tried to process what had happened. But, before he could fully register the first attack, he was slammed back into the wall. He could feel his bones grinding under his skin, "So Vyom, how was it? Jus' like the old days, eh?" Nera Vesper chuckled.

Arjun's head spun, his vision blurred, and his breath came in ragged gasps. Focusing was nearly impossible, especially with Nera Vesper preparing for yet another strike. But, just as Nera Vesper lunged, Arjun abruptly dropped to his knees and drove his right leg diagonally into Nera Vesper's right ankle, sending him crashing face-first to the ground. The crowd held its breath, their silent cheers heavy in the air.

Humiliated and stunned, Nera Vesper stared at Arjun, struggling to determine whether the boy before him was truly just thirteen-year-old or something far more formidable. Unsure, he made a move to stand, but before he could rise, a firm hand held him back.

Nera Kashyap stood seething, "Enough" He hissed, Then turning to the tense students, he barked "Class Dismissed".

==============================XXXXXXXXXXXXXXXXXXX=========================

After more than an hour of driving through the dimly lit, stranded streets, Thoris was still searching for a place to stay the night. Little did the old General know, securing an accommodation in this small village at such a late hour was next to impossible.

For a brief moment, he even considered turning back to Simla, but the faint sound of a radio in the distance gave him hope. Partially obscured by thick branches, fluorescent green neon sign flickered- Subedar da Dhaba.

Subedar Bruno Singh, the bar's owner was a pleasant-looking military veteran, "What can I get you?" He asked, scratching his bald head.

"Just a chilled beer " Thoris replied, his eyes scanning the modest establishment. With only four or five mostly unoccupied tables, the place was small and untidy. At the far end, sat an old man glued to a little television mounted on the column, his lips firmly attached to a bottle of cheap vodka.

"It's all chilled around here" Bruno chuckled at his own joke, "No freezers needed in this sort of weather". He poured the beer into a tall glass, "To be honest, I thought you would ask for something stronger" He confessed with a sheepish grin.

"Given up long back" Thoris smiled dryly, making an awkward attempt in conversing. He had never been good at chatting.

Bruno grinned, rolling up the sleeves of his faded red shirt "I can't believe you just said that to a bar owner! Had you been a tad louder, you might have ruined my business." Then with a curious tilt of head, he inched closer. "So, what brings you to Nagvari, business or pleasure?"

"Both! At my age, business is the only pleasure I have left" Thoris took a sip, wondering whether or not to ask about Arjun, but decided against it. It was wiser to not raise suspicions.

"Come on, you look far too fit for your age" The man remarked.

"My age tells me I should be in bed rather than chatting with strangers". Thoris quipped "Speaking of which, do you know where I can find a decent hotel at this hour?"

Bruno sighed. "I am afraid there are no hotels here. But if you drive about seven or eight kilometers down the highway,y, you will find a flashy inn called Grizzlies"

Thoris raised his brows. "Grizzly? As in a bear, right?"

"Yea," Bruno chuckled, "Grizzlies stands at the very spot where its founder- a well-known hunter in these parts- killed a big grizzly bear with his bare hands"

'Not another village legend' Thoris groaned, "I suppose Grizzlies it is then" he handed a five hundred rupees note to Bruno.

Bruno rummaged the cash drawer. "I don't think I have enough change at the moment" He sighed, "Can I return it to you tomorrow?"

"Don't bother" Thoris said, knowing well that the small sum he was paying Bruno was worth way lesser than ndothe information he would back here for later, "Keep the change" He smiled.

Grizzlies wasn't exactly "flashy" as how Old Bruno had described it.

A weather-beaten standee featuring a large, black bear, the words G-R-I-Z-Z-L-I-E-S falling out of its blood-stained mouth, confirmed that this was where he would be spending his night.

Inside, the reception area was poorly lit, its rough green walls adored with a framed photograph of a stocky, bearded man in a black suit, holding a rifle in one hand and a bear's severed head in the other- undoubtedly the inn's famed founder Bruno had mentioned. Beneath the frame, a pot-bellied man in an oversized brown coat and an beige woolen cap was snoring heavily.

It took Thoris two full rings of the service bell and a vigorous shake to rouse him, The man blinked drowsily; his breath reeking of cheap alcohol.

"What?" He grunted.

"Room"

"How many?"

"One"

"Five thousand advance" To Thoris's astonishment, for the first time, the man spoke a full sentence.

Thoris handed him the cash, well aware he was being overcharged, but too exhausted to protest.

"Ramesh" The man croaked at a lanky teenage boy, standing outside "Show him to room number 102."

The room was as modest as rest of the inn.- a small table, a rickety chair, a single bed with a worn-out white bed sheet, couple of hard pillows, and a thick blue quilt.

"Need anything else?" Ramesh asked with a coy grin.

"Not now, thanks" Thoris replied, handing him a hundred rupees note as the boy opened the door.

As soon as the door closed, Thoris wasted no time. Carefully, he pulled out a nearly torn, pastel-colored manuscript wrapped in a cellophane bag. The ancient manuscript, coated in dust, looked as if it hadn't been opened in centuries.

Handwritten in patrician cursive, its title read, "Auronteolan Faunanticso" (Advanced Faunatics)

===============================XXXXXXXXXXXXXXXXXXX=========================

If Parth hadn't fetched Nera Kashyap on time, Arjun would have been squashed- or at least, that's what Parth had believed. He had quietly sneaked out of zone 1 to find Kavya but stumbled upon Nera Kashyap along the way. Yet as always, the outcome of their contest had taken an unexpected turn!

However, it appeared that Arjun's latest encounter had earned him far more admirers than Parth had anticipated. To say that Arjun was met with a "few" handshakes, whistles, and war whoops could have been a gross understatement. The reaction were nothing short of overwhelming. But, who could blame the students? After all, it wasn't everyday a first year student single-handedly defeated a much despised top ranking professor.

"Silence!" A loud voice cut through the commotion.

A stout women in a silver jacket and matching knickers stood staring at them. Her short, dark hair cut short, contrasted against her tanned skin, making her appear even more formidable.

"Who is she?" Parth whispered to the short Japanese student standing beside him.

"Nera Nehatara. She is our fencing Professor"

"She fences?" At almost six feet and two hundred pounds, Nera Nehatara was hardly the image of an agile swordswoman.

"You" She said, pointing directly at Arjun, "I have heard about your little duel with Nera Vesper. Your friends may see you as some kind of hero". Arjun stared at her, taken aback as she shook her head in disdain, "But, I am not so lenient as him".

"Who says he is a hero, Nera Nehatara?" A sharp voice suddenly rang out.

A tense silence swept the room, as the students instinctively parted, paving the path for a cat-eyed boy about their age. His light brown hair styled in sharp porcupine spikes, uneven at the edges, and slightly tweaked near the temples. His small nose twitched sideways with every word he spoke. In one hand, he casually balanced a helmet, while his other hand held a slender gleaming sword.

"Here comes the Devil" The Japanese boy gritted his teeth.

"Who is he?" Arjun turned to ask, but the boy had already stepped back.

"Why ask the chicken? I will tell you" The boy roared, "My name is Manuel Domar, Junior Grade fencing champion- three years running" the boy announced, "I presume your name must be trickster". Arjun blinked at him, caught off guard, "What else would you who cheated to win?" Manuel scoffed, smirking.

Arjun couldn't fathom what he had done to deserve such disrespect. It had only been two days and yet, it seemed like almost everyone in this school despised them.

"How dare you make such a remark?" Parth snapped; his temper flaring at the insult to his friend.

Manuel's expression turned venomous "Because I know your kind" Manuel smirked again, "poor, hungry, uncultured Anva...." He never got a chance to finish, Arjun seized Manuel by the collar; his jaw clenched tight.

"Manners, both of you" Nera Nehatara called them to order, cutting through the tension.

Just then, the school bell rang, much to everyone's relief.

<h1 style="text-align:center">VII</h1>

Secret of the Southern Banks

The first few days promised an action-packed future, but the weeks that followed felt dull in comparison. Aside from occasional clashes with Manuel, who they later discovered was Neratara's son life settled into a routine.

Strangely enough, even Nera Vesper had kept his distance from the boys after their first class with him. He still took occasional jibes whenever he got a chance, but largely chose to ignore them. Fencing, on the other hand, turned out to be surprisingly easy- though it would have been much easier without Manuel constantly getting in their way. Still, his arrogance and their infrequent duels were the very things that kept the boys motivated.

Their biggest concern, however, wasn't Manuel or Nera Vesper, but their academics, where they still struggled to find their footing. Santosh excelled in Survival Strategy and more often than not Arjun and Parth relied on his notes to keep up. But, with the first quarterly tests only a month away, Parth was determined to make a mark academically; while Arjun, true to his form, remained either unfazed or at least pretended to be.

By March, the quarterly tests had arrived at Gurukule! Santosh and Liam spent countless hours helping them catch up (and yes, by then, the boys learned the Japanese student's name- Liam Chew, Santosh's roommate). During exam days, food and sleep became secondary concerns. Parth and Liam managed to get through with reasonable accuracy, while Santosh was competed for the top percentiles alongside Manuel and Reema Bhatt, the petite, studious girl in their class. But, it was Arjun whose indifference startled everyone; no matter how hard or easy the questions were, he never discussed his tests.

==============================XXXXXXXXXXXXXXXXXX=====================

By April's end, the quarterly tests finally concluded!

Their first class after the grueling exams was History. As usual, Nera Norton whispering voice filled the room, and today, he was in a mood to assign projects.

"Mr. Chew and Mr. Grill," He announced, handing a sheet to Liam and Kenneth Grill, the sandy-haired class prefect. "Your topic is The rise and fall of Yevusa, the King of Native Spain'"

"Ms. Bhatt and Ms. Ryder, your topic is Contribution of Neartic Region to the ancient world". He handed another sheet to Reema. Reema's face lit up. It seemed she had received the topic of her choice. Her partner Suzan Ryder, a chubby Aussie girl with long, middle-parted blonde hair was happy that her partner was happy. Then again, anyone paired with Reema never complained- She was a complete bookworm, and all her teammates had to do was to carry photocopies of the assignment that Reema had so diligently prepared.

Nera Norton glanced at the two remaining sheets in his hands, he shook his head quietly as he took another look at the papers, "Mr. Kumar and Ms. Feathers, your project is Atlantis, the lost city'". He handed one of the remaining sheets to Shrey Kumar, a stout boy with red cheeks, and short white hair; he was Manuel's best friend, and yet another snobby *Big Shot Anvantaras*", while his thoroughly uncomfortable looking partner Betsy Feathers was a thin Afro-American girl with sharp cheekbones and a nervous smile.

"And the last topic for the day," Nera Norton swept a quick glance over the class, "The story of The Mighty Vyom Vardhan' goes to...." He took a moment to recall their names, "Mr. Anand and Mr. Mehta." Although, Nera Norton's body language and behavior suggested the otherwise, but the boys couldn't help wonder if they were deliberately assigned this topic.

"Let me remind you all" He added, his voice barely rising. "This project accounts for one fourth of your annual grades. So make it worth every mark"

History classes at Gurukule had always followed a set pattern, but that day something unexpected happened. Just as he was about to leave, Nera Norton stopped, turned and for the first time in their stay at Gurukule- smiled at the boys.

"As for you two," He whispered, "this project has the potential to shape your destiny, so do it well...*really* well"

==============================xxxxxxxxxxxxxxxxxx========================

Little did they know, the Vardhans Nera Norton spoke about were not just another family, they were royalty in the world of Anvantaras.

Vyom Vardhan was one of the greatest and most legendary Anvantaras of modern times and his bloodline remained as distinguished.

His great grandson, Vivek Vardhan was a person of exceptional skill and more importantly, the Nera-in-chief of the famous Gurukule before Nera Bramhashiva. But, it was his daughter who was truly destined to rule.

Veera Vardhan was a prodigy. She mastered level 8 of Advanced Arms Combat at the age of six, and by fifteen she had likely mastered more than two third of the Anvantaras capabilities.

==============================xxxxxxxxxxxxxxxxxx=====================

By the time Thoris finished reading the first three chapters of the manuscript, the sun was already high over his head. The worn-out white curtains did little to block the blinding sunrays, reflecting off the ice-covered driveway, but he felt too lazy to complain. The past two days had been exhausting- first, the grueling training with the elephants, followed by an almost day-long journey to Nagvari. Fatigue weighed heavily on him. Without much thought, he threw a bedsheet over the worn-out curtains, desperate for some much-needed rest.

A buzzing phone jolted him awake. A private number flashed on the screen, "Hello" Thoris mumbled groggily.

"How have things been?" came a deep, familiar voice.

Thoris struggled to place it, "Who is this?"

"Tvashtar"

It was as if a bucket of cold water had been dumped over him. Sleep vanished instantly. Thoris couldn't be any more awake, "H-His Highness". He fumbled, taken aback by the unexpected call from his King, "I am tracking the boy in Nagvari. I plan to use a few unconventional methods to find him."

"Like what?"

"Faunatics" He said hesitantly, unsure if Tvashtar could even recognize the term.

"You mean the ancient Korean trackers' art of using animals to find people?" There was a subtle hint of excitement in Tvashtar's voice. Clearly, his King was more knowledgeable than Thoris had assumed.

"Yes, Your Highness"

"But, I thought nobody had used that method in over a thousand years"

"That's true," Thoris admitted. "But I was fascinated by it in my youth, so I studied it extensively. Although I have forgotten some parts of it over time, but I can revive it"

"Good" was all Tvashtar said before the call ended.

Thoris sat still, staring at his phone. Why was his king so obsessed with avenging his brother? Was it truly out of genuine fondness or was there something deeper he didn't know? As far as he could recall, Ankara had never mentioned any closeness with Tvashtar.

==============================xxxxxxxxxxxxxxxxxx====================

The sea stretched endlessly before her, glistening under the bright sun. The waves rolled gently, their rhythm steady and calm.

Standing on the cliff, Veera stared at the horizon, her heart pounded with anticipation. Somewhere beneath the vast ocean lay her destination- a hidden temple said to hold the one of the three mythical seals her grandfather had spoken of.

But how was she supposed to find the temple beneath the sea. Unsure, she reached into a small leather pouch fastened around her waist. There was a family heirloom. She pulled it out and stared at the ornate looking golden compass intently. The needle trembled, pointing ahead. Without hesitation, we descended the cliff and stepped onto the boat moored in the sea.

After what seemed like hours, she saw a massive whirlpool in front of her. He glanced at the compass one last time. It was blinking incessantly.

At the center of the whirlpool, a shimmering portal appeared, rippling like liquid glass.

She missed a pulse. This was the portal, the *veil*- the entrance.

The temple will test you- Her father's words echoed in her mind.

Without hesitation, she gripped the oars tightly and steered the boat straight into the swirling vortex.

The moment her boat entered the vortex, everything changed. A strange sensation washed over her- like an eternal timelessness. The sky, the sea, everything blurred into shifting colors and shadows.

Then with a sudden jolt, she landed on the other side- a land!

The world before her was unlike anything she had ever seen. The sky was deep brown, streaked with golden clouds. The water beneath her feet was smooth and dark, reflecting the sky like glass.

And in a distance, rising from the water, stood what looked like an ancient temple, its stone walls covered in moss, worn by time.

The temple will test you- Her father's words once more echoed in her ears. But this time they had more to offer- *"It will show you your fears and doubts. You have to stay strong, Veera*

She swallowed hard.

There was no turning back now.

===============================XXXXXXXXXXXXXXXXXXXX=====================

Facing the wall, he stood in silence, staring at the reflection before him- a worn-out disheveled man he barely recognized. Seven days at Grizzlies without proper sleep or a decent shower had left his eyes bloodshot and swollen.

"Long time, no see" Bruno recognized his generous customer.

"Got anything to eat?" Thoris asked, wondering whether today was the right time to bring up Arjun.

"Nothing fancy" The old man replied, "Just Paratha and Dal"

"That will do"

Bruno signaled to a young, ill-dressed boy to fetch the meal, "So, how is Grizzlies treating you?"

"Overpriced, but decent"

"Yeah, that son of his, all he does is hog and hap" He referred to the drunk receptionist cum owner disdainfully..

Thoris leaned in slightly. "Can I ask you something, Bruno?"

"Tell me"

"Have you heard of a boy named Arjun?"

Thoris' question was well timed as the meal arrived. Bruno nodded. "Yes, a fine young lad, and his father, what a man! Mr Mehta was the kindest and bravest man, Nagvari has ever known" Bruno poured himself some cheap rum, its stench filled the air between them, "But then fate struck and everything changed".

"What happened?"

"A fire broke out at their house one night" Bruno downed his rum in one swift gulp, "And the Mehtas were caught inside".

"What caused the fire?"

"Nobody knows for sure. There are plenty of theories, but no real answers. It seemed like some freak accident"

Thoris swallowed hard, his heartbeat quickening "Was the boy caught in the fire too?" He fought to keep his voice steady. Was his quest finally coming to an end?

"No, he was in Mumbai the time, studying but" Bruno paused to pour another drink.

"But what?"

"But after his parents died, the boy simply disappeared" Bruno whispered.

Thoris stared deep into Bruno's eyes, trying to decipher what might have been left unsaid. "Just like that?"

"Yes, just like that" Bruno sipped his rum, "But tell me, where did you hear about him?" Bruno asked, stirring the dal with his thick fingers.

"At the inn" Thoris lied smoothly, "Someone was telling the same story." He reached into his pockets. "Thanks for the lunch, Bruno."

"No, this one is on me" Bruno grabbed Thoris' hand with a firm grip, "hope you don't mind?"

Thoris offered a small smile, "Just one last thing, Bruno?"

"Tell me"

"Where can I find birds here?"

Bruno looked back, startled

"I am an ornithologist, I study birds" Thoris laughed, masking his lie.

'But I don't see a camera" Bruno said, scratching his bald head.

"I am an ornithologist Bruno, not a wildlife photographer. I study birds in their natural habitat- I don't shoot them with cameras" Thoris laughed even louder to camouflage this lie as well.

It worked. Bruno flashed a toothless grin. "My bad. We get to see so many camera people around here- I thought you were one of them" He wiped his hands on his apron. "For birds, drive north, the woods are up ahead".

==============================XXXXXXXXXXXXXXXXXXX=====================

The entrance to the temple, an ancient gateway was partially submerged in the dark waters. The towering stone structure were adorned with intricate symbols, glowing under the shadows of the dim twilight.

The temple has a will of its own. The deeper you go, the harder it will be to keep your mind clear. It won't offer easy answers. It will test you- your fears, your desires. If you succumb, you can never leave. The words kept flowing.

Veera tightened her grip around the hilt of her knife, another family heirloom. Taking a deep breath, she stepped inside the temple.

Inside, the air was thick, heavy with the weight of forgotten time. A suffocating stillness filled the place, the damp scent of the ancient stones adding to the mystery. She was sure faint whispers slithered through the silence, though no other living soul was in sight. The chamber stretched endlessly and its towering walls lined with small, glowing holes that appeared like watchful eyes.

Are these the voices? She asked herself.

Ignore them, focus. The voice in her mind resurfaced

She pressed forward, the corridor narrowing as she ascended a spiraling staircase carved into a rock. With each step the air grew colder, the whispers more insistent.

You won't succeed. It was her father's voice again, but not the usual encouraging one. She strained her ears.

Veera… This time it was her mother- Soft, familiar. Calling to her. *Do you hear me?*

She nodded without thinking.

You think you are worthy of retrieving the seal- That you are the next Vyom Vardhan? No, you are nothing but a disappointment, a girl pretending she belongs in a world of men. You won't succeed Veera. I tried. And you know what happened to me. The temple will never let you win. Go back or you will lose yourself forever.

A lump formed in her throat. Her mother- here? Not possible. His rational mind rebelled, but the yearning in her heart wished it was true. Her foot moved of its own accord, drawn towards the sound.

Veera no, don't listen to the temple. It knows your weakness. Her father's voice again cut through the fog in her mind.

Veera blinked. Shaking off the trance. Her heart sank as she realized how close she had been to giving in. The temple just wasn't aware of her- it was toying with her mind.

She ascended further, but the whispers never ceased. Instead, they grew more personal, more intimate, calling to her in voices she trusted. Fragments of childhood, memories long buried- surfacing with painful clarity. She clenched her fists, trying to shut it all out, but the temple knew where exactly to strike.

The last staircase ended, opening into another chamber. Inside, an imposing stone altar was placed in the center of the chamber, atop the altar lay a single object- a small intricately carved stone tablet.

"The Third seal" She breathed, her eyes fixed on it.

Once you take this, there is no turning back. The temple will resist you. Breaking the seal, will awaken it fully"

"I am ready" She inhaled sharply and steadying herself.

She placed her hand on the tablet.

For a moment, nothing happened.

Then, with a deafening crack, the tablet split.

===============================xxxxxxxxxxxxxxxxxx=====================

Thoris pulled up right beneath the hill. Quickly, he climbed his way to the top. His gaze sweeping across the vast forest beneath. *"If I can see the forest from here, the forest can see me too"*. Thoris muttered, his eyes narrowing as he studied the area.

Slowly, he shifted his weight onto one foot, crossing the other leg over his knee in a Faunatics position. Folding his hands over his head, he commenced chanting – first, in a soft tone, then, gradually raising his voice, *'Breaeeoeoo suyuaapap lipa aajauyai treeetam thutha thuthe digyaram volavurum (I have come this far to seek thee.… Help me o' those who can run, swim, or fly)*

His chants grew louder, echoing through the wilderness. Seconds melted into minutes and the minutes became hours, yet he remained unmoved, his voice resonating into the depths of stillness around him.

===============================xxxxxxxxxxxxxxxxxx=========================

Lima had insisted that it was easiest history project ever. After all, the Mighty Vyom Vardhan was nothing short of a legend at Gurukule. There wasn't a record that he hadn't broken, if not created during his time there.

It was a Friday evening and the orange sun outside their window was busy draping the dark blanket of the night when they heard Santosh yelling all the way down from the hallway, "Guys?"

"Now what?" Arjun groaned.

"The results are out!" Santosh burst into the room, sweating.

"And?"

"I didn't top" he admitted with disappointed sigh.

"Who did?" Parth asked, secretly praying it was not Manuel!

"Reema Bhatt" Santosh sighed.

"And your score?"

"Ninety-five, she beat me in Modern Warfare" Santosh muttered.

"And you are complaining about that?" Arjun growled.

"What about Manuel?" Parth' priorities lay elsewhere

"Seventy-eight" Santosh chuckled.

"Even that's pretty high" Arjun sighed, "What about me?"

"Sixty-four"

"And that's bad, right?" Arjun glanced at Santosh.

"Not as bad as you think" Liam grinned, entering the room.

"How about you?"

"Seventy-nine"

"And me?" Parth finally realized he hadn't asked about his own marks.

"Seventy-three" Santosh read from his palm, where he had scribbled down their grades

"Bravo Parth" Arjun patted Parth. Liam chuckled. "Wait, does that mean I failed?" The realization dawned upon Arjun.

"Forty-five is the passing grade, you passed with flying colors, mate" Liam reassured him.

"But" Santosh interjected, "Parth and Arjun, you need to work on history and modern warfare, you two have barely passed in these two papers. And almost all outdoor subjects for Liam" Santosh reminded them.

"History won't be an issue." Parth said confidently. "Liam says we got the easiest project in class- The Mighty Vyom Vardhan".

Santosh shot Liam, a long, unimpressed look.

"What's wrong?" Arjun groaned.

"The Mighty Vyom Vardhan is considered the toughest topic of modern history" Santosh revealed.

"Huh?" Even Liam couldn't believe what he had just heard.

"People only know about his early life. What happened after he left Gurukule and before his meteoric rise remains one of the greatest mysteries of the modern Anvantara World"

The revelation stuck the boys like lightning. Mediocre grades, the toughest project, and clueless lives. Nera Brahmashiva had been right - their fates were indeed their foremost foes!

"But guys, listen" Santosh said, noticing their disheartened expressions, "My dad knows a bit about the Mighty Vyom Vardhan, Maybe he can help you both with your project" Santosh smiled, "So let's see, if you do well in your project, it will cover one fourth of your marks". Santosh was already busy calculating their grades on his fingertips, "And modern warfare is more aptitude than memory, so all you need is a bit more practice...."

"Ok, it is settled then," Liam said, eager to move on. "What do we do now? It is Friday evening- Recreation Center?"

"No," Santosh frowned, "Library"

"Library?" Liam and Arjun chorused in disappointment.

"Yes. We need to help Parth and Arjun with their history project, besides Liam, lets not pretend you are at top of your class" Santosh said, unapologetically.

===============================XXXXXXXXXXXXXXXXX=========================

The temple roared around her. The ground beneath her feet trembled, but she stood firm, her hand clenched tightly around the fractured tablet.

The energy from the shattered altar pulsed through the air, lingering like an echo. The whispers returned, softer now, but their tone shifted- less haunting, more curious.

It's not over yet. The voice inside her mind said.

Veera's heart raced, the weight of the temple's gaze heavy on her shoulders. It knew her weakness, her uncertainties. But, she stood her ground, and now felt stronger, more in control.

It's waiting for you in the final chamber.

The whispers around her had dulled, but the weight of the temple's presence was still palpable. Cautiously, she ventured deeper. With each step, the air grew colder, the shadows thickening around her, as if she was descending deeper into the very soul of the temple itself.

Her hands stretched, her eyes adjusting to the evolving darkness. Her fingers brushed something metallic. A tingling sensation shot through her hand. With a deep breath, she pushed. Slowly, the door began to creak open, revealing a dark, hollow space beyond.

This was the largest chamber yet. Its ceiling lost in the shadow. At the far end, suspended in midair, was a massive orb. Its surface rippling and shifting like liquid smoke. Veera could feel the raw power radiating from it- the heart of this temple, the source of its strength- the seal!

And, in front of the orb, stood a figure.

===============================XXXXXXXXXXXXXXXXX=========================

No one typically spent their Friday evening in a library- especially, not after results had just been declared; but Santosh sadly was different.

Moving from shelf to shelf, book to book, the boys searched for anything that mentioned Mighty Vyom Vardhan. It was not an easy task in the sprawling, three-story grand central library, which housed well over a billion books.

And Santosh was right. Records on Vyom Vardhan were scare. After what felt like an eternity- four grueling hours- the boys finally headed back to their rooms, carrying only thirty books on the legendary Anvantara.

Santosh wasted no time, organizing a rigorous study plan. Each book had to be thoroughly read and notes were mandatory.

"Be careful with your writing Liam" Santosh scoffed as the boys reached Shaantilok. Liam's writing was notoriously illegible, a wall of text with no punctuations in sight.

Santosh, unsurprisingly, was the first one to return the fourteen books- Nine of his own, and five of what Liam had inflicted on him. His notes were amazing, detailed yet concise; no wonder he was one of the toppers!

Parth was still through his fourth book when a small note fell out of the book. Curious, he picked up the neatly folded white paper.

'Greetings Parth & Arjun,

By now, I hope you must have realized that Vyom Vardhan just wasn't another Anvantara, he was a legend! If you want to know how he became one, meet me at midnight by the southern bank of the dark lake. May be once you know how Vyom Vardhan became a legend, you would too realize why you are expected to be another"

Parth breath hitched. He passed it to Arjun. Together they read and re-read it. The writing seemed excruciatingly familiar, only if they could recall where they had seen it.

================================XXXXXXXXXXXXXXXXXXX=========================

As the southern shores of the dark lake stretched beyond the city of Neranche, it lay outside the protection of the city's thermostatic atmosphere, which shielded the rest of the city against the harsh Himalayan weather. But, it wasn't the weather alone that posed a threat. This monstrous water body, infamous for its extreme salinity, and pitch-dark water was also rumored to be haunted. However, the real challenge for the boys wasn't the dark lake or its eerie reputation- it was their escape from Gurukul. The humungous gatekeeper of Gurukule, was notorious for his vigilance and fiery temper.

For the first time in months, as Arjun pulled out the fur coats from the cupboard, he felt a strange excitement stir within him. It was as though they were about to embark on a secret expedition, though his heart was equally filled with fear. He knew this was a big gamble for them. Being caught meant end of their plans. No one was allowed beyond the Gurukule gates after dusk and the southern banks of the dark lake were strictly off-limits even to the final year students.

It was an odd sight- those formidable gates of Gurukule, unmanned and wide open. Never in the history of the institution had they heard of such a thing. Even the scary gatekeeper was mysteriously absent, though whether it was deliberate or coincidental, the boys didn't have time to consider. It was already nearing midnight, and they had to reach the shores before the clock ran out.

================================XXXXXXXXXXXXXXXXXXX=========================

It was like a human- but larger than any person Veera had ever encountered. Cloaked in a flowing black robe, it seemed to merge with the shadows around it. Its face was hidden beneath a hood, but even from within the darkness, two glowing eyes stared directly at her.

The guardian of the temple.

Her stomach twisted. How was she supposed to defeat something like that?

It's a force- an embodiment of the temple's will. You can't fight it with strength alone. You must outlast it.

To her horror, the figure slowly began to move- gliding towards her without a sound. The air grew even colder, and the shadows around it thickened.

All her instincts screamed at her to run, but there was nowhere to go. She drew her knife and took a step forward. As the figure approached closer, the whispers returned, louder and more venomous than before- doubt, fear, regret- all the emotions she had been trying to suppress came flooding back.

"You are weak, Veera" The whisper hissed. *"You cannot win. You will fail, just as your mom once did"*

Veera clenched her jaw, fighting against this relentless tide of negativity. Her vision blurred as the figure drew closer, wrapping around her like cold chains. But she refused to give in. She had come too far.

The figure stopped just inches from her face. Its glowing eyes piercing through the darkness. It raised one hand, and without warning threw a spear at Veera.

Time seemed to slow down as the spear approached her. Her body moved instinctively, raising her broad knife to block the blow. The spear clashed against the blade with a deafening roar, the force of the impact nearly knocking her off her feet. Her arms trembled from the strain, but she held her ground, refusing give up.

The figure tilted its head, as if surprised by her resistance, and pulled back the spear. But it wasn't done. More shadows erupted from its form, lashing out at her.

With a loud shout, she pushed forward, slashing her knife through the shadows, cutting through the cold darkness. Each strike felt like a battle against her own doubts, own fears, so she pressed on.

The figure hesitated, its glowing eyes narrowing. The whispers grew louder, more anxious, but something had shifted. But the harder she fought against the shadows, the more the temple's ancient power weakened, its strength draining with every strike she made

Keep trying! This is the end.

Then, with a blinding flash of light, the figure shattered. A thick, ominous cloud of dark smoke surged upwards, ripping through the ceiling, shattering the temple's stones in its path.

The air cleared, and for the first time since entering the temple, she could breathe freely.

The first rays of dawn peering through the damaged ceiling suddenly unlocked the pattern on her tablet, as if there was an invisible lock. The pale stone gleamed gold as the inscriptions on the seal grew legible.

Congratulations Veera!

==============================XXXXXXXXXXXXXXXXXXXX==========================

The southern banks were completely deserted. Not a soul in sight, not a single movement. All they could see was the thick fog and hear was howling of the freezing Himalayan wind. The infinite stretch of the dark waters meet the moon at the horizon, gave the lake an ominous presence.

"Are you sure this is the place?" Arjun finally broke the silence, his eyes scanning the empty shores.

"The letter said so" Parth muttered, rubbing his gloved hands vigorously for warmth

Arjun frowned. "What if this was one of Manuel's tricks to get us expelled" The thought hit him suddenly. "Think about it- he was the one who distracted the Gurukule gatekeeper and then opened the gate through some hidden lever."

Parth hesitated. "Maybe you are right. Manuel can pull something like this. And if anyone at Gurukule discovers we are gone-" He stopped, his face growing pale. "What if Manuel has already brought Nera Brahmashiva and other Neras to the gate? What if we have already been? But will we be reprimanded publicly, or simply asked to leave?" Parth just couldn't stop talking

"Shut up Parth" Arjun snapped.

"No seriously Arjun, what do we do now?"

Arjun glanced at his watch. It was 12:09 AM, "Maybe we should just go back and hope this was not a set-up"

Without another word, they turned back, carefully retracing their steps through the dense fog.

"Move faster," Parth had at last spoken something that wasn't gibberish, "The wind is picking up".

==============================XXXXXXXXXXXXXXXXXXXX==========================

At first, it felt nothing more than a strong gush of wind. But, when it started following them, that they knew something was wrong.

Hovering about fifty feet above them, a monstrous figure loomed in the dark sky. The full moon cast a halo around its serpent-like head, which sat atop a long thin neck. Its eyes like burned like molten lava, its pointed mouth gleamed with rows of long sharp teeth. Two tiger-like clawed feet gripped the ground tight, its tail similar to that of crocodile, trailed behind. The rugged scales on its body and two sets of fluorescent yellow wings right behind the small, clawed hands, were convincing enough to make it a monster.

Parth and Arjun would have sprinted faster than Olympic athletes- only if their legs weren't frozen in fear. For a long moment, they stood paralyzed, too terrified to even breathe. But they managed to move, it was already too late.

The monstrous creature emerged from the water with terrifying speed, half flying and half running, cutting off their escape. Its yellow wings slammed down like walls on their sides, leaving them with no choice but to face the creature, only if they knew how?

Lured by the expectation of easy prey, the creature's claws went shot forward, sinking deep into the flesh of his right hand. Arjun let out a sharp cry as he collapsed on the ground, pulling Parth down with him.

His entire body shivered. His fingers seemed to have touched something- cold and metallic. Through the corner of his eyes, he saw it- a long silver sword. Arjun was certain it hadn't been there moments ago. Someone had deliberately thrown it, and the roaring wind had masked the sound. However, whoever it was, wasn't stepping in to help. The boys had to fight for themselves.

With his uninjured hand, Arjun grabbed the sword and swung it at the creature. The blade stuck- but barely scratched the creature's thick, scaly hide. Instead of harm, it only seemed to amuse the creature. It reared on its hind legs, its clawed hand seizing Arjun from the ground, its blazing eyes fixed at the little human who had dared to challenge it. The silver sword slipped from his grasp, as the grip tightened around Arjun.

================================XXXXXXXXXXXXXXXXXX==========================

Parth saw the opportunity Arjun had missed. He lunged for the fallen weapon, but the creature was faster. Its long tail lashed out, sweeping Parth off his feet. The sharp scales tore through his fur pants, slicing into his leg. Parth was bleeding. He tried to stand up, but his legs refused to hold his weight. Before he could react, he was rolling down the steep shore- straight into the freezing depths of the dark lake.

Satisfied with its first catch, the creature turned back to Arjun. Its forked tongue lashed out as if savoring its prey. Arjun closed his eyes in submission and almost immediately opened them back.

For a split second, he thought he was hallucinating- until Parth actually swung the sword. It was then Arjun realized it was happening for real! The blade barely nicked the creature's leg, but it was enough. The Beast stared down, acknowledging the second threat.

The tail lashed out again, but this time, Parth was ready. He leaped aside, avoiding the deadly strike. The creature dropped Arjun, shifting its focus to the new challenger.

Its outstretched forelimbs swiped at Parth but missed, as he dove out of its reach, just in time. The irate beast hesitated for a moment- A brief pause that was the first stroke of luck the boys had all night. Seizing the opportunity, Arjun quickly joined his friend, finally giving them the opening they had been desperately waiting for!

Timing their jump to perfection, together they pierced the sword deep into the creature's underbelly- the one place where its scales were thin and vulnerable. The sword slid in effortlessly. The creature let out a blood-curdling cry, plunging into the sea. The icy waters from the impact left them both drenched.

But they didn't care. They had won.

Or so they thought.

A bright flash of light erupted from the depths, illuminating the entire shore! Their blurred eyes took time to adjust, but what was unfolded before was beyond their wildest dreams. They watched in stunned silence as the dreadful creature transformed into a beautiful young woman, then, at once, aged into a graceful, old lady.

================================XXXXXXXXXXXXXXXXXX==========================

The world around Veera blurred again into a swirling vortex- she felt as though she was falling, tumbling through space and time, the ground beneath her vanishing into nothingness.

Suddenly everything stopped, she found herself sitting in a familiar room. She blinked, disoriented, as she realized she was back home- in the Vardhan Palace.

Her father, Vivek Vardhan in a formal Nera attire, stood in front of her, his expression unreadable. "Welcome back"
She folded her hands and greeted him.

"The seal, please" She handed the seal to her father. He studied it intently. His polished, bald head reflecting the light emancipating from the golden seal. "So what did you learn?" He glanced back at Veera.

"There is a way to get *him* out of the void" The void was a place of eternal nothingness where neither light or time could reach.

"But the cost is unimaginable." Vivek groaned bitterly. "The equation of this world we know will change forever"
Veera glanced up at him. "This is the only way, and you know it"

================================XXXXXXXXXXXXXXXXXX==========================

"I don't know how to thank you boys" the woman's swollen red lips parted into a gentle smile, her voice as smooth as silk, "Don't be scared, I am not your enemy" The lady inched closer to them, her long grey tresses flowing with the wind.

"Not our enemy?" Parth scoffed, "What kind of person devours boys our age?"

"Only a cursed Piorotaur could commit such a dreadful act" came a familiar whisper. Before they could even place the voice, the green-eyed woman rushed into Nera Norton's embrace.

"Nera Norton, how could you do this?" Arjun demanded. Nera Norton lowered his eyes as the truth dawned upon the boys. It was Nera Norton who had assigned them the history project on "The Mighty Vyom Vardhan" and deliberately left that cryptic note in one of the books.

"Boys, I know what he did was wrong, but trust me, his intentions weren't" the lady said, taking a deep breath, "It was our tenth wedding anniversary, and we were celebrating by the lake, I believe our laughter must have drawn the hermit to us." Her beautiful face turned somber as she gazed at a distance, lost in the painful memory, "The hermit told us he had been meditating deep in the caves and that our presence disturbed him. He ordered us to leave at once…."

"…..But the Anvantara in us wasn't used to taking orders, especially not from a Human" Nera Norton continued, "I, in particular, gave him a piece of my mind about how to treat a woman, and then I committed a grave mistake…." Nera Norton glanced at the lady, his eyes filled with regret. She placed a comforting hand on his shoulder "I mocked him about the pleasures of love, something he had denied himself in his pursuit".

"And this enraged the hermit." She said, her voice was hoarse with emotions, "He cursed me- my beauty that my husband was so proud of. The curse turned me into this hideous creature. And so, for almost five hundred years I have lived in this wretched form"

"Is that even possible?" Parth asked skeptically, "Turning someone into a creature with just a curse? And how can somebody live for five hundred years?"

"Seers and hermits possess ancient magic," She explained. "Their curses are incredibly powerful. And as for age, Anvantaras can live well beyond thousand years. The oldest recorded was a Mongolian Anvantara, born around the same time as Jesus, and had lived for over twelve hundred years!!!"

"But why didn't you apologize to the hermit" It was a simple question from a fourteen-year-old boy.

"We did," She said softly. "We pleaded. But a curse once spoken cannot be undone. However, seeing our grave remorse, he revealed that only a true *Al-athanan-* a star-marked soul could break it"

"And one of us is that Al-athanan?" Parth asked.

She nodded. Parth was about to ask something else, when Nera Norton suddenly beeped. "Time to leave boys".

"With her?" Parth asked, bewildered. Sneaking back into Gurukule was already risky enough- returning with a mysterious woman in tow seemed like a sheer madness.

"Yes with her," Nera Norton replied, a hint of amusement in his voice. "And her name is Nera Aisha Brahmashiva Norton"

"Wait" Arjun's eyes widened. "Even the Head of Gurukule is a Brahmashiva".

"That's because Nera Aurochitra Brahmashiva is my brother, Arjun" A smile played at the corner of her lips.

================================XXXXXXXXXXXXXXXXXXXX=========================

His eyes nearly bulged out, even through the heavy armor, as the weight of the new revelations hit him. First, Nera Norton had appeared unannounced in dead of the night with a complete stranger. Second, he wasn't alone- he had Parth and Arjun with him.

"What are you two doing at this hour?" The guard snarled, assuming that Near Norton had caught them sneaking out.

"They are with me" Nera Norton stated firmly, crushing the guard's hopes of seeing the boys punished.

"And the lady?" He pressed, still skeptical

"She is Nera Brahmashiva's sister" Parth was happy to answer that. The guard almost bowed at the revelation.

Quietly, they followed Aisha through Gurukule's hallways. She moved with a familiarity that made it seem as though she had left.

"Come in" They heard the familiar baritone.

"Brother" Aisha tightly hugged Nera Brahmashiva.

To Parth' surprise, even the ever-composed Nera Brahmashiva didn't attempt to hide his emotion. They held onto each other for what felt like an eternity, "Five years Aisha, five hundred years since that dreadful day" Nera Brahmashiva murmured, pressing a kiss on her forehead.

"Thanks to these boys" She said, beaming at them.

Nera Brahmashiva turned to Arjun and Parth. His eyes filled with gratitude, "I am deeply indebted to you both for breaking the sister's curse. But, tell me which one of you did it?" Though he asked but there was knowing sparkle in his gaze- he already had the answer.

"He did" Both the boys almost spoke together, pointing at each other.

"I didn't, you did Parth" Arjun insisted, "My hands slipped off the handle when we jumped"

"But how could have I done it? I barely had any strength left. I still have the wounds from her attack" Parth rolled up his trousers to show the deep gash, only to freeze in shock, "How is it possible, it was just here" Parth couldn't believe what he was witnessing.

"Parth, did you get wet at any point?" Nera Norton asked, his voice thoughtful.

"Yes, she knocked me into the lake with her tail" Parth glanced at Nera Isabella.

"That explains it"

"Explains what?" Parth asked, still puzzled.

Before an answer could come, Nera Brahmashiva intervened. "It's late, boys. Time to return to your rooms" He said with a firm yet kind smile. "And thank you again"

The boys exchanged glances. It was clear they wouldn't get any more answers that night.

As they walked away, Parth caught the last thing spoken before the door closed behind them-

"What else must he master brother, before we can be certain he is the *one*?"

VIII

Faunatics

The soft flutter over his shoulders pulled him back to reality. A tiny sparrow perched near his ear, chirping softly, its innocent eyes gazing at him.

'So after all these days, it was just a lone bird I could draw,' he thought glumly to himself!

But the deep snort of a beer proved him wrong. What lay ahead of him was nothing short of astonishing – more than a hundred animals and birds stood or sat facing, waiting in absolute attention.

"Wlayatey; untriono sthrotio Arjun mred rosstan rindhio

Trata joiyuo droma noure hoyoma

Phujo kolo pika sio notru gapoo dio"

(Out there in the world, search for Arjun all around,

No matter if it's sky, water or ground,

Find him amidst songs of his might, for if you trace him down;

Make sure he is never out of your sight

Float me the news at the very break of the dawn

And I will there before he is gone")

Thoris addressed the gathered creatures in *Faunatica*- an ancient language that could command every animal in the world. To his relief, the moment he concluded, the animals dispersed, a sign they had set off on their mission.

Yet, Faunatics, had two significant limitations, often referred to as *twel pleomas, or* the *two bindings* - The first, the summoner had to **remain** at the very spot where the command was issued. Leaving it, for any reason, would render the command void. The second- the summoner had to **adhere** to a strictly vegetarian diet, ensuring that his food choices did not offend the very creatures whose help he sought.

Though Thoris had no idea how long he would be bound to this place, two things were clear - first, he needed food to survive, as he hadn't eaten since that last lunch with Bruno, and second, he needed shelter.

It took over three hours of meticulous foraging through the dense forest, before he managed to find some wild edible mushrooms- his only source of food amidst a forest teeming with toxic herbs, plants and fruits. The mushrooms were damp and tasteless, but then he had no other choice.

Building a shelter, however, was a simpler task. As an ex-army man, constructing a temporary refuge came naturally. He set to work, breaking sturdy branches, gathering mud and layering them over the hill. He made a quick run down to the nearby shallow stream, filling his boots with abundant water, and pouring it over the dry mud to create a firm foundation. The four of the sturdiest branches that he collected were driven into the wet mud, ensuring they would tightly hold firmly once it dried. The remaining branches were used to form a makeshift roof and walls.

By the time Thoris finished his little shack, the forest was pitch black.

==============================XXXXXXXXXXXXXXXXXX=======================

It was a fresh beginning. His office was unusually organized and he sported an entirely new look. The scruffy beard was gone, and his long unkempt hair had been fashionably combed into long tresses. Even his clothes looked new. It was a striking transformation- from his earlier unkempt self to a refined gentleman.

"Good morning, boys" Nera Norton beamed; their only disappointment, his voice hadn't changed. "You have been called here for a reason" He continued, "But before I reveal it, tell me- how is your history assignment progressing?"

Arjun frowned. "You give us the toughest topic, send a Piorotaur behind us, and still expect us to answer"

Nera Norton chuckled apologetically. "I know boys, it had to be done. And, that's exactly why you are here, for some damage control" He flashed a sheepish grin. "I want to send you both to someone, who is an expert on Mighty Vyom Vardhan".

The boys exchanged wary glances. The last time, Nera Norton had 'helped', they had barely escaped a Piorotaur. What could possibly be in store for them this time?

"Mr. Natarajan- a Gurukule alumnus, and a close friend of Vyom Vardhan has agreed to assist you".

"And where do we find him?"

"At Jalsthal, Gurukule's school swimming pool!" Nera Norton replied. "It is right across the Central Office. Mr. Natarajan is usually there between three and five in the afternoon".

===============================XXXXXXXXXXXXXXXXXXX=========================

The survival strategy class felt dull and boring, compared to the anticipation brewing inside them. After all, it wasn't every day that they had the chance to uncover all the mysteries surrounding the Mighty Vyom Vardhan.

Their first visit to Jalsthal was a striking reminder that mediocrity had no place in the Anvantara world. Calling it mere swimming pool would have been a gross understatement- it was more akin to an endless river. Its vast expanse stretched so far that one couldn't see from one bank to other. The pearl blue waters shimmered like an immeasurable silk, its edges ruffled gracefully with the beautiful, white waves.

"Watch out, boys?" A voice yelled, shattering the stillness of the place. The abrupt warning startled Arjun, who was leaning forward to admire the crystal-clear depths. Losing his balance, he tumbled headfirst into the depths.

===============================XXXXXXXXXXXXXXXXXXX=========================

"A shark in fresh water?" was Arjun's first reaction as he spotted the familiar fin slicing through the surface. His instincts kicked in immediately, and he frantically picked up speed, but the shark was far quicker than he had anticipated. The massive bluish-gray shark, nearly the size of a bus, moved with terrifying agility. It shot towards him like a torpedo, its long, protruding teeth gleaming beneath the water.

Dazzled by fear, Arjun managed to swim out of its way, just as the giant creature whizzed past him, leaving behind white bubbles, on its trail. But his relief was short-lived. The shark had already turned around, and every time Arjun moved an inch, it mirrored him with unsettling precision. Soon it was clear how difficult it would be to escape its relentless pursuit.

For a moment, they were both still, watchful but motionless. Then, Arjun lunged forward and grabbed its right fin, and twisted it with all his strength. A sickening snap echoed through the water- the fin broke under the pressure! With a violent jolt, the shark flung him away. Thrashing in agony as blood gushed from the fresh wound. Wounded, it retreated into deeper waters.

With a war whoop, Arjun lunged out his head, and he saw them- ten other fins were quickly converging on him, drawn by the scent of blood!

IX

Allakaadd

Scared, he glanced back at the shore; it seemed so far away. His hope briefly sparked when he spotted a distant boat drifting across the Jalsthal, but that too dwindled as the boat sailed away, leaving him surrounded by a dozen, hammer-faced sharks, steadily closing in.

"If you can turn your biggest weakness into your greatest strength, Arjun, no one can defeat you" He heard his Nera Reran's lesson echo in his head. Promptly, he asked himself what was his biggest weakness? His Size - only if he was bigger and mightier, the sharks wouldn't have attacked, but his small size meant...a faint smile crossed his face!

The closest shark lunged at him, but Arjun swiftly swam diagonally, grabbing hold of its fin. The massive fish tried to jolt him off, but Arjun clung to it with all his might.

The boat was clearer now, it sailed right towards him. But still it was too far.

===============================xxxxxxxxxxxxxxxxxxxx=========================

Arjun twitched its fin slightly and the shark jolted, moving a little in the direction of the twitch to ease its pain. Arjun smiled to himself as he twitched the fin a bit more; this time in the direction of the boat. The shark headed straight for the boat. Arjun repeated the exercise, every time the shark seemed to lose momentum or focus. Each such attempt brought him closer to the boat. On the deck, an anxious looking, middle-aged man, likely Mr. Natarajan, stood next to his equally worried best friend. But, what startled Arjun most was the sight of Nera Reran at the wheel, sailing the boat toward him. He never thought he would be so glad to see Nera Reran!

Nera Reran handed the wheel to Mr. Natarajan and leaned forward, dropping a small, green bar into the water. It created a pale froth and the shark began dispersing swifly.

"Let go off the shark" Nera Reran yelled in his nasal tone, his voice sounded more like a whistle than a command.

Arjun obediently released its fin.

"I am sorry." Arjun gasped as Mr. Natarajan pulled him to safety on the deck Nera Reran gave him an incongruous look but continued driving, this time toward the shores.

"Tell me, how did you manage to escape the sharks on your own?" Mr. Natarajan asked, both stunned and impressed.

"Just followed my instincts"

"If we hadn't reached on time" Nera Reran scoffed from behind the wheel, "that might have been your last tryst with those instincts"

"But technically speaking, Arjun alone bailed himself out. We only found him to our credit Nera Reran" Mr. Natarajan corrected.

"But...how come there are sharks in sweet water?" Arjun asked, still perplexed by what had just happened.

" Jalsthal is used for a sport called Allakaadd." Mr. Natarajan explained. "It's an Anvantaras versus wildlife sport. The sharks are bred in fresh water for this game."

"Allakaadd?" Parth asked, confused.

"It means *Primal Game* in the ancient language"

Suddenly, Nera Reran stopped the boat in middle of the water and turned to them as if stuck by a sudden revelation, "Mr. Natarajan, did you just say that this boy alone managed fight off the sharks?"

Mr. Natarajan nodded.

"What's your name, son?" Nera Reran's voice softened like a cotton.

"Arjun"

"Which wing?"

"Shaantilok"

"Is it?" His face lit up, as resumed the driving the boat, "Follow me to my office, now!" The last part came out rather sternly; Mr. Natarajan excused himself for other chores. In the meanwhile, a group of paramedics in their beige jumpsuits rushed past them to tend to the injured sharks.

"Just you" Nera Reran pointed at Arjun, just as Parth followed his friend

===============================xxxxxxxxxxxxxxxxxxx=========================

Shoddy was surely the adjective that best described his office.

Papers and files strewn everywhere, dusty white curtains dangled from the windows, and wooden cupboards were cramped far beyond their capacity. It was more cluttered than even Nera Norton's office.

"Find a place to sit boy" Nera Reran said.

Arjun brushed aside a pile of papers off a chair before sitting down.

" I am not sure how much you know about Allakaadd" Nera Reran said, settling on his chair stiffly, "Its a game where the most powerful creatures on earth- the Anvantaras take on the most dangerous creatures of the water- the sharks. As for the rules of the game, Miguel explain them to you".

"But why are you telling me all this?" Arjun asked, confused by Nera Reran's unexpected interest.

"As the Nera in charge of Shaantilok, I would like to nominate you as an Allakaadd Advancer for our wing".

"Advancer? B-But" Arjun tried to protest. He didn't understand why he was being dragged into a game of which he hadn't even heard before! But he also knew that it was pointless arguing with Nera Reran.

"I know a talent when I see one, Arjun. Now go, don't you have other things to do?"

===============================xxxxxxxxxxxxxxxxxxx=========================

"What did he say?" Liam asked the moment Arjun stepped out of Nera Reran's office.

"What are you two doing here?" Arjun looked at Santosh and Liam, surprised to see them waiting outside.

"We were passing by and saw Parth. So we stopped." Santosh replied. "Now, what did Nera Reran say?"

"He wants me to become a Shaantilok Advancer"

"No seriously?" Santosh nearly shouted in disbelief, "Do you even realize how big that is? I can't believe that you have just joined the ranks of the elite!" Santosh looked ecstatic "In the last two thousand years, only four Anvantaras from junior school have made it to the Allakaadd!"

"And who were they?" Parth asked, turning to at Santosh

"Nera Brahmashiva, the Mighty Vyom Vardhan, Veera Vardhan, Vyom Vardhan's great-granddaughter and now Arjun. But, Arjun has been nominated in his first year, which is a record in itself" Santosh said, practically beaming.

===============================xxxxxxxxxxxxxxxxxxx=========================

After changing into a pair of comfortable denims and a white sweatshirt, Arjun headed straight for the cafeteria. The entire ordeal had left him starving. The large whiteboard over the buffet counter announced today's menu-Chinese. Scanning the room for familiar faces, he found none except for Parth, who sat in a distant corner, quietly devouring his dinner. Arjun joined him. Parth gave him a slight nod; it was evident that the food was too good to be interrupted.

"Are you Arjun?" Someone tapped his back

"Yes" Arjun turned around to see a senior boy with short black hair.

"Hi, I am Miguel, Miguel Fraga. I assume Nera Reran spoke to you?" Miguel extended his hand, "Mind if I join you?"

"Not at all" Arjun said, shaking his hand.

"So tell me- have you played or even heard about Allakaadd before?" Miguel asked, placing his plate on the table.

"No, but Nera Reran wants me to play as an Advancer" Arjun said, slurping a noodle into his mouth.

"Well, before I explain the game, let's cover the basics" Miguel began, "All four wings participate: Shaantilok, The Capers of the south wing, The Artics of the north wing, and Techonova of the west wing. The game is played at Jalsthal- the freshwater lake you saw earlier." He took a sip of his cola before continuing, "Each team is assigned a fixed position on one of the lake's four sides of Jalsthal, marked by their respective flag." He turned to Arjun, as if preparing to say something important, "The teams are divided into Advancers, Thwarters and Defenders. The Jalsthal serves as the battlefield, with a red flag positioned at its center. The Red flag is worth a hundred points, while each team's individual flags placed at their respective corners are worth twenty-five points each. The objective is simple- teams compete to capture as many points as possible and the one with the highest points emerges as the winner"

"Is there a time limit?" Arjun asked.

"Yes, three hours. The game always begins at dusk"

"Why after the sunset?"

"To increase the difficulty, of course! Besides," Miguel lowered his voice, "though I probably shouldn't be telling you this... as your captain, I think you should know- no team has captured the red flag in the last thousand hundred years"

"Not even Veera Vardhan?" Parth asked, surprised.

Miguel shook his head.

"Why?"

"Ah, I forgot to mention a small twist" Miguel said with a smirk.

"Which is?"

"The red flag is guarded by deadly sharks"

"That explains the sharks" Arjun murmured.

Miguel nodded as he continued with his meal.

"But what are roles of the advancers, thwarters and defenders?" Parth asked.

"Glad you reminded me! Nera Reran would kill me if I forgot that" Miguel chuckled.

Parth smiled.

"The Advancers are responsible for capturing flags- whether it's their opponents or the red flag. Thwarters on the other hand are tasked to avert the attack from the Advancers from the opposing teams. And lastly, the Defenders make sure their team's flag stays unconquered. Before I forget- one last thing you should know" Miguel smiled mischievously.

"And that is?"

"The sharks are free to attack anyone."

"What a relief!" Arjun growled, raising his eyebrows.

Miguel burst into laughter.

"Tell me Miguel, am I the only Advancer from Shaantilok?"

"No, each team has eight players, three Advancers, three Thwarters and two Defenders. You will be playing with alongside Larry and Vijay as your fellow defenders."

"What position do you play?"

"I am a Thwarter"

"If you don't mind me asking, who was the last person to conquer the red flag?" Parth looked at Miguel curiously

Miguel smirked. "Isn't it obvious?"

"The Mighty Vyom Vardhan?" Arjun asked.

Miguel smiled, "See you tomorrow in the Shaantilok recreation center, seven pm sharp"

==============================XXXXXXXXXXXXXXXXXXXX========================

Nera Kashyap announced his arrival with the towering stack of papers. "What's wrong?" He asked.

Nera Brahmashiva was restlessly pacing in his large office- an unusual sight for someone always composed.

"It's Arjun", Nera Brahmashiva said, darkly, "Someone is trying to find him"

"Don't we already who know?" Nera Kashyap sighed. He didn't understand why Nera Brahmashiva seemed so troubled over the obvious!

"It's not Tvashtar. I have sensed the birds searching for Arjun."

"The birds?" Nera Kashyap gave Nera Brahmashiva a bemused look.

"Yes" Nera Brahmashiva took a deep breath, "Faunatics is an ancient Korean Tracking art" Nera Brahmashiva walked over to his favorite spot- the French window, "The Trackers use this art to seek help from the animals to track down their subject"

"How I have never heard of it?" Nera Kashyap mumbled.

"That's the real concern. Faunatics hasn't been used in like over a thousand years. It's a lost art"

"Then who is reviving it?"

"That's exactly what I am trying to find out through Reverse Faunatics"

"You know Faunatics!" Nera Kashyap's eyes widened.

"Of course," Nera Brahmashiva said calmly. "I was once a Tracker, Nera Kashyap"

==============================XXXXXXXXXXXXXXXXXXX=========================

"Are these real sharks?" Parth whispered to Liam.

"No, mechanical ones, but equally dangerous."

"Advancers, Thwarters take your positions" Miguel yelled as he entered the water alongside his fellow Thwarters- Neil and James. Arjun stood behind the other advancers Larry and Vijay as they took their stance. From the banks, Parth and Liam watched alongside the Defenders.

"Ok Arjun," Larry said. "In case you don't know the rules, an Advancer has to muscle his way either to the central platform, or to the opposing team's flag, whichever is more convenient or closer" He pointed towards the red platform in the center, where Miguel stood with James, and Neil, the other two Thwarters.

"On my command boys... Three Two One.... Go" Miguel shouted as the sharks neared.

Vijay was the first one to make a move. He swiftly both Neil and James, by diving underwater and then resurfacing at regular intervals. His speed left the two thwarters- James and Neil momentarily stunned.

Just ten feet from the platform, Vijay noticed a shoulder glistening next to him. Before he could react, Miguel seized him by his waist and effortlessly tossed him back to the starting point. He crashed into the water with a loud splash.

"Larry, you are next" Miguel yelled.

Larry was a seasoned player; he carefully swam towards the Thwarters. Neil was the first one to confront him. Neil swung his heavy arm, which Larry dodged as he jammed his right fist into Neil's stomach; Neil retreated holding his stomach, his face wincing in pain. James, however, was ready. He brought down Larry with a huge leap. As they wrestled mid-water, both appeared evenly matched. But when Miguel joined in, Larry was suddenly outnumbered.

Still Larry, wasn't one to go down without a fight. Regaining his balance, Larry thrust his left hand into Miguel' chest, twisting it anti-clockwise. Miguel yelped in pain, managed to still throw his fist at Larry, but Larry swiftly bent back. Turning on his heels, and he grabbed Miguel by the waist and flipped him over his back- Miguel crashed straight into the James.

With all three Thwarters down, Larry swam towards the platform. Just as he in an arm's distance from red flag, the entire pool area boomed with long mechanical shrieks, followed by a short one.

"Three to one" Liam groaned

"What?" Parth looked at him.

"One short shriek means Larry landed one hit, while three long shrieks mean the sharks hit him three times. That means Larry is out... he lost three to one"

"But can't he rejoin the game?"

"No, three shark hits automatically disqualifies the player." Liam explained

"But this is unfair" Parth protested. "what if the player is willing to fight back"

"The rule was introduced in the interest of the players. Three shark hits are what an average Anvantara can take, without being fatally injured"

"Not bad Larry! Arjun warm up" Miguel called, rubbing the red lump on his chest.

Arjun wiped his hands nervously on his shorts and dived. He thought he had tricked Neil, but as soon as he surfaced, a well-aimed hook sent him flying backwards. "And you thought I was that dumb?" Neil teased.

Arjun managed a weak smile before disappearing underwater again.

This time, he aimed for James. James was prepared, but rather than attacking James, Arjun zipped past him at an astonishing speed. Neil reacted quickly, swam diagonally to cut Arjun off. But Arjun had already seen him coming; with a thin smile he waited till Neil got closer, but his smile faded when he saw Miguel closing in fast from the other side.

Arjun didn't panic. Instead, he adjusted his plan. Miguel and Neil assumed Arjun had frozen under pressure, charged towards him. Just as they neared, Arjun shot upwards like a dolphin, causing the two Thwarters to collide underwater.

Done with the Thwarters, Arjun now swam towards the platform. Seeing a fin approach, he carefully approached the steel-colored animal. Mustering all this strength, Arjun delivered few powerful punches on its iron cast body. His fist ached, but the speaker blared with two short shrieks.

Under the water he hadn't noticed two more sharks, quickly closing in. The first shark dug its metallic teeth into his right hand's flesh; the speaker let out a long shriek. Arjun fiercely swung his right hand, but the heavy machine barely moved under the water; even the other shark was now dangerously closing in. He took a deep breath, and with all his strength, Arjun swung his right hand hard enough that the shark went crashing into the other closest shark; although the sound of metals clashing muffled under the water but the impact drenched the spectators on the banks. The speaker buzzed with multiple short shrieks, leaving the baffled audience wondering

Just a shark away from the platform, Arjun cautiously swam forward. Only a few feet remained. He scanned the water for any sign of danger, but everything seemed clear. Satisfied, he threw his hands on the concrete platform, and almost at once rolled back into the water, unconscious. The last thing he remembered was being hit by a train!

Arjun woke up in the infirmary, staring at the empty, white beds around him. "What happened?" He mumbled

"Where have you been, buddy?" Larry beamed, "I mean, seriously, knocking two Thwarters, and three sharks in your first training. That's insane!" Arjun noticed his Allakaadd teammates had gathered around his bed.

"But what exactly happened to me?" Arjun repeated

"You were hit by the Shroger" Ryan, the quiet, broad shoulder defender, replied.

"A what?"

"A Shroger is a leader of the shark pack. It is generally more powerful than the rest and....." Sigourney, another defender, paused

"And?" Arjun pressed

"And.. only a lucky few survive a Shroger hit without broken bones"

"Now we know why Nera Reran wanted you so badly on the team" Larry added with a sheepish smile.

"How did the others fare?" Arjun asked, trying to sit up.

"Good, but nowhere close to you" Miguel helped him up, swiftly slipping a pillow behind his back

"Actually, what Miguel meant" Nera Reran interjected as he entered the infirmary, "is that after your performance, no else dared to go near the sharks"

"When will I be discharged Nera Reran?".

"In a few days"

================================XXXXXXXXXXXXXXXXXX=======================

"Wake up Parth" Arjun shook Parth, "We are going to be late".

"It's Sunday, Arjun" Parth groaned, rolling over his back.

"I am going to Jalsthal to meet Mr. Natarajan. I was told he would be here this morning" Arjun reminded curtly

Parth bolted upright, his sleep gone. They still had a billion unanswered questions about the Mighty Vyom Vardhan and their last meeting with Mr. Natarajan had ended with Arjun

joining Shaantilok's Allakaadd team as their star Advancer.

================================XXXXXXXXXXXXXXXXXX=======================

They found Mr. Natarajan sitting by the Jalsthal, engrossed in scribbling notes into a small, spiral notepad.

"Morning, Mr. Natarajan" Parth greeted.

"Morning boys" He responded absentmindedly, his eyes still on the notes.

"I believe Nera Norton spoke with you" Arjun said as they settled beside him.

"Oh yes, you have some history project on..."

"On the Mighty Vyom Vardhan" Parth finished.

"That's right" Mr. Natarajan set aside his notepad, "So what do you want know?".

"Everything"

"Hmmm, where should I start?" He scraped his knuckles in thought, "I suppose from the very beginning"

The boys leaned in, listening intently.

"Ok," He sighed, "Twelve hundred years ago, a boy was born in the Famous Vardhan family- the first son after two daughters" He paused for a moment to think, "The Vardhan family was one of the oldest and most respected Anvantara families. Sir Veer Vardhan, Vyom's father was the chief advisor to our then King," He shifted slightly, stretching his legs for comfort, "Vyom grew up in a highly disciplined environment. He was just five, when he was inducted into Gurukule, and it didn't take long for everyone to notice his brilliance. The Gurukule's corridors buzzed with tales of his intelligence, benevolence and courage". He chuckled softly. "Vyom you see always had a knack to help others. He didn't care who they were, as long as someone needed him. Being a Vardhan, bravery and benevolence ran in his blood."

"May be that's why Vyom Vardhan was the youngest Anvantara to play Allakaadd" Parth remarked.

"One of the youngest, Nera Brahmashiva was the first one to set the record of being the youngest Anvantara to play the primal game" Mr. Natarajan corrected, "Anyways," He continued as if he was never interrupted, "Over time, Vyom only improved; being revered everywhere for his qualities" Mr. Natarajan gulped, "He was like what, some twenty three old when he got an offer from the palace to join the King's army! Can you believe an offer from palace, at that tender age?"

"Which King?"

"His Royal Highness Hryiterehan, the father of our current ruler, His Royal Highness Tvashtar"

"Anvantaras have their own King?" Parth seemed surprised.

Mr. Thompson nodded.

"So where did you meet Vyom Vardhan?" Arjun asked.

"At Gurukule, right?" Parth guessed.

"No, I first met Vyom in the army" Mr. Natarajan disagreed with a quiet smile, "It was the celebration of His Royal Highness Hryiterehan's three hundredth year of coronation, and forces from all over the world had gathered". He turned towards the deep placid blue waters of Jalsthal, as if reading from its infinite vastness, "I commanded the Western Regiment, when I was first introduced to this young man who was chosen over me to lead our regiment's procession. My sources confirmed that he was the Chief Advisor Vardhan's son." He smirked, shaking his head "My first impression of him? A privileged snob who had wielded his father's position to take the my opportunity. To be honest I wasn't particularly polite to him" Mr. Natarajan's face frowned

The boys listening, wide-eyed.

"It wasn't until the Thanksgiving Ball I learnt his full name- Colonel Vyom Vardhan. To this date, I regret my immature behavior towards him".

The boys shot him an astonished look

He smiled at their puzzled faces, "You see, Vyom Vardhan was already legend in the army. The youngest Colonel in the army history. A war hero. An ace sportsman. A generous philanthropist. And he had earned it all without ever using father's influence" Mr. Natarajan looked away, "That night, during the Ball, I apologized to him. He had never needed his father's influence- his own name alone carried more weight than the combined achievements of many of us".

The boys exchanged glances, their respect for Vyom Vardhan, growing with each word.

"Our interactions increased when, two years later, he was appointed King's Commander in the West. It didn't take me long to realize why this man was such a trusted aide of the crown..." Suddenly, Mr. Natarajan stood up.

"Are you leaving?" Parth asked, disappointed.

"I have a very important meeting at the Central Office" He smiled apologetically, "Can we continue his on Wednesday?"

"Next Wednesday!!" The boys chorused in disappointment. Three whole days felt like an eternity of waiting!

"I am sorry, but it's important, boys" Mr. Natarajan shrugged, Then, he turned towards Arjun, "By the way, how's your training going, Arjun?"

"Good except for the occasional brushes with the Shroger".

"Stay safe" Mr. Natarajan wished and meant.

Parth and Arjun resentfully traced their path back to Shaantilok. Miguel was waiting for them outside their room, "Arjun, the training sessions are being expedited. Nera Reran says we need more practice, meet me at the Recreation Center in ten minutes"

The Allakadd training sessions grew more intense with each passing day. Arjun struggled to balance the grueling practice alongside the academics. Meanwhile, Mr. Natarajan sent a word on Tuesday- he was travelling to India for urgent business and wouldn't be back until Christmas.

===============================XXXXXXXXXXXXXXXXXXX=========================

Her mind was already racing ahead, calculating, planning. The Void must be breached, but how?

"The Allakaadd is tomorrow" Her father's voice tore through her thoughts, as he entered her room.

She glanced at him absentmindedly. "I won't be able to make it, Father"

"You know it's a tradition we must uphold" He said firmly.

She pushed back her dark hair, still lost in thoughts.

"We are going tomorrow, please be ready" He reiterated before turning to leave.

Veera remained unconvinced. But perhaps, it wasn't a bad thing after all. She couldn't breach the void alone- she needed allies. Maybe Allakaadd would let her shortlist potential talent.

But even then, the path to breaching the Void was a long and demanded so much more.

===============================XXXXXXXXXXXXXXXXXXX=========================

"Phew" Arjun whistled as the Shaantilok Team made their way towards Jalsthal. Adorned with round, glowing yellow lights, the path to Jalsthal had never looked more beautiful- glowing yellow lights lined the entrance, casting a warm hue over the cobblestone. Even the otherwise boring Greek foyer at the entrance of the Jalsthal was embellished with yellow lilies and frills.

Inside, the stadium was altogether another spectacle- The towering, multi-tier stands were packed to capacity. Hence finding any empty seat truly needed a giant stroke of luck. The East, West and South stands buzzed with excited students, while the relatively smaller North stand was reserved for senior Neras and dignitaries.

On the first row, Nera Brahmashiva sat in deep conversation with elderly, bald headed Nera, whom they had never seen before at Gurukule. A few rows behind them, Kavya, dressed in white Nera overalls, sat next to Nera Michelle. Yet, Parth's eyes drifted elsewhere- drawn to a strikingly beautiful, tall, dark-haired girl, seated in the first row to the new Nera, who was chatting with Nera Blinzerberg. She exuded an aura of quiet power.

Beneath the grand arena, water looked marvelous- it's pearl blue color sparkling under the soft glow of the underwater lights.

The visible edges of Jalsthal, four small platforms proudly displayed the flags of each wing. The white platform, at the topmost right corner belonged to The Artics, the sky blue on the bottom right was for Techonova, the light orange in topmost left had Shaantilok's flag, and the green located in the bottom left was occupied by the defending champions, Capers. The competitors stood poised at their respective ends, their swimming trunks and tees matching their platforms.

Parth slid into a seat in the seventh row of the west stand. Santosh and Liam had already secured spot beside them, their eyes glued to the spectacle unfolding before them.

With a thunderous buildup from the orchestra, the legendary red flag platform was unveiled in style. The stage was set for the primal game!

"Nervous?" Kumar glanced at Arjun as they took their positions, standing seventy feet away from the imposing red platform, at the center.

Arjun nodded, exhaling slowly "You?"

Kumar gave a quiet smile.

"Welcome to Jalsthal, my friends" Nera Brahmashiva's powerful voice resonated across the stadium, "And, Happy Annual Day everyone" His voice had a slight hint of pride, "We all know, in 4987 BC this great institution was founded by Nera Bharat. Since then, we have celebrated twenty third November as our Annual Day." His gaze swept across the audience- some seemed cheerful, some sober, but all listened in rapt attention. "Thirty-five years later, in 4952 BC, just like so many of the young faces here today, five young Anvantaras dared to challenge the deadliest creatures of sea, creating a game we now call Allakaadd." Parth leaned forward, mesmerized by Nera Brahmashiva's command over history. "In 4942 BC, a decade later, Gurukule became the first school to officially include Allakaadd as a major sporting event". He swept another glance over the stands, "Although Gurukule Day has a plethora of events showcasing the brilliance of our talented brigade, I think we can all agree- nothing, absolutely nothing is a more befitting finale than Allakaadd". The audience erupted into a thunderous applause, the Nera Supremo smiled. "So, without further delay, I officially declare the Allakaadd OPEN!!!" A wave of excitement washed over the stadium as the announcement echoed through the air

"Thank you, Nera Brahmashiva" Nera Keith Marshall, the freckled, elderly Nera Parth met on his first day at Gurukule, assumed the role of the event's anchor, "Ladies and Gentlemen. Let me quickly recap the rules, though most of you already know them" He grinned, prompting a ripple of laughter from the audience. "As you can see, each of the four teams is stationed at their designated platforms. Each team is classified into Advancers, Thwarters, and Defenders. The red flag at the center is worth a hundred points. Each individual team flag is worth twenty-five points each. The one with highest points is the winner." Nera Marshall took a dramatic pause. "Now that we are clear....." He raised his voice above the mounting roar, "......Release the sharks. Let the mayhem begin!"

==============================xXXXXXXXXXXXXXXXXXXX==========================

Nathan Richards and Leonard Miles took their positions in the north stands as commentators. Nathan, a former Artic captain adjusted his mic, whiles Miles was a third-year graduate and an expert on Allakaadd scanned the stands with a smirk, "Ladies and Gentlemen, Girls and Boys, tighten your seatbelts- there is going to be turbulence in the water" He chuckled.

Nathan rolled his eyes. "Miles, spare them the comedy. I think the game would be cracking enough" He snapped jovially.

"Sorry guys, looks like Nathan lost his sense of humor on the way here- anyone who finds it gets free Capers merchandise" Miles quipped before his voice turned serious, "Oh and look at that! The Techonova Advancers are already heading straight for the North- Artics platform"

Nathan's voice rose in excitement, "Bold move! I wouldn't bet against Billy, the Artic Thwarter. He is phenomenal. The West wing miscalculated- Techonova Advancers have made a wrong move"

Miles shook his head, his eyes locked on the pool, "I don't think so. Look at the Techonovan Advancers- they have split themselves into two units. That's the strategy, Nathan" he brought the microphone closer to his mouth, "Here goes your chance, Nathan! Your girl Your boy Billy has been bullied and even the other Thwarters- Rufus and Siobhan have also been dislodged after some heavy-duty punching. Bianca Maxfield, this Techonovan Advancer, continues to impress even this year, she has already knocked off two Thwarters single handedly".

"I feel there's still hope," Nathan said as if he was trying to reassure himself, "Come on, guys, put up a fight". He groaned aloud in frustration as both Arctic Thwarters and Defenders were trampled by the Techonovans. Bob Summers, the Artic Defender was the only guy trying to put up a fight, but Bianca was way too much for all of them. Her muscles throbbed as she greeted Bob first with a straight hook, doubled it up with a right cut, and the lethal kick to the jaw finally finished Summers off. It was a one-sided contest, The Artics never stood a chance.

"The Techonova will soon have their first points of the day" Miles observed

"Hold on! That's Jovan Raj in the house and he is heading for the kill" Nathan shouted. The entire stadium seemed to shift their attention. Jovan Raj, the estranged son of General Kofi Raj, with his unmistakable ginger hair and imposing presence, surged through the water at a terrifying speed, who was advancing towards Shaantilok, suddenly sped back towards the rattled Artics flank. The other two Advancers from Southern wing Capers too followed him in close pursuit, "Gear up Techonovans, *Raj* is coming."

"Jovan Raj certainly is the best Advancers of our times" Miles agreed, "I mean just look at the way he swims, I have never seen anybody swim faster my entire life!!"

"And he kicks hard too" Nathan chuckled.

"Techonovans and Capers headed for a clash for that icy Artics Flag" Miles gritted his teeth, "Nathan, you think Techonovans have a chance now?"

"As long as the Capers are not playing Jovan Raj"

Raj's teammates engaged the Techonova's Advancers, while he himself lunged at the Artics' flag. Bianca, the burly Techonovan Advancer, sprang onto the platform to confront the ace Caper Advancer.

"Okay, the first major action of this evening, and what better opponent than Bianca," Nathan was euphoric, "the Techonovan Advancer swings her fist wildly at Raj, and she misses...." A few sighs emerged from the western stand.

"But Raj doesn't; he isn't the best Advancer for no reason, Nathan" Miles remarked, "The famous *Caper Advancer* has been unleashed" Raj blocked in Bianca's fist with one hand, and doubled it on Technonovan Advancer's face with the other. The muscular Techonovan Advancer tried to come back after the initial blows, her knees went up, but Raj blocked them with his elbows and in a rough tackle, thumped Bianca's face on the ground, unconscious.

"Bad luck Bianca" Nathan sighed.

Raj swiftly removed the white flag from its post and waved it at the crowd. The crowd roared, chanting his name. The Points Tally flashed twenty-five points for the Capers.

Nathan chuckled, "Man, doesn't the crowd love him!" The crowd continued chanting Raj's name.

Miles' eyes squinted at the water, eyes narrowing, "Wait, why is Shaantilok still holding back? With Techonovan Advancers out, Capers is now their major opponent and this certainly is not great news if I were a Shaantilok fan".

Then, as if on cue, there was a movement near the eastern platform.

"Arjun, aim for the red flag," Miguel whispered, slicing through the water "Larry and Kumar are heading for the Techonovan Flag".

The commentators noticed immediately. "Who is that kid?" Miles asked, watching Arjun dive under the water.

Nathan burst out laughing, "Looks like Shaantilok swapped their drawing team for their Allakaadd team". His voice was taunting, "No wonder they are lying low".

But Miles wasn't intrigued, "The Shaantilok Advancers, Larry and Kumar, are making a move toward the depleted Techonovan flank, clever".

Nathan grinned, "My friend, don't get ahead of yourself. Techonovan Thwarters are led by Vladimir Ulrich and I still haven't forgotten last year's Allakaadd. He took down Raj." Miles was right, Techonovan Thwarters were better than Larry had anticipated. And call it their misfortune, a large pack of sharks too were circling them to play the spoilsports.

"We have our first Shaantilok casualty, Kumar" Miles sighed. Kumar couldn't match up to the swelling shark attack; he hadn't even reached the Techonovan platform, when he was cornered by a pack of sharks. But, the Shaantilok Advancer didn't go down as easily as Nathan made it sound; he still tackled the sharks valiantly even when they were digging into his limbs.

"But, at least, he scored some points" Nathan noted at last.

"Let's see" Miles replied, "Wait, isn't Larry in your class?" Miles looked at the lean Shaantilok Advancer with interest, "He is super agile, man!"

"Yeah, he is" Nathan nodded, "Don't be fooled by lean frame, Miles... that's just a disguise for the great strength that lies beneath".

"Hmm, look at the way he is devouring the Techonova Thwarters" Miles gaped, "In the last three years, I have never seen Vladimir being so badly manhandled. And that stomach move of his, man, it looks lethal".

Nathan exhaled. "Seeing him in action makes me wonder, if it is his fault to have been born in the same era as Raj".

"Well, that's too overrated, don't you think?"

"Maybe you are right" Nathan admitted.

Miles smiled, "I think your friend Larry has messed up at last" His eyes set on the match, "I mean, it's ok that he is strong and skillful, but engaging all the three Techonova Thwarters at once, well that's not clever". He sighed, "And he is panting, clearly running out of breath".

As if sensing the desperation of his ace Advancer, Miguel whispered something to Sigourney, as he himself headed toward the blue Techonovan platform.

"Now that's interesting!" Nathan observed with amusement.

"What?" Miles stared. He hadn't seen Miguel swimming across to the Techonovan flank.

"This is a most unusual role reversal" Nathan said, his voice still amused, "Miguel it seems has assumed the role of a full-fledged Advancer and...."

"And joined Larry" Miles completed the sentence, equally astonished "I mean really gutsy move" he remarked admiringly, "No one can think of a role reversal at this point of game".

"Me neither, it's like expecting Raj to play a defender" Nathan grinned.

"Well talking of Raj" Miles said, "He noticed the Techonova flank in distress. Look, he is signaling his team. The Caper Advancers are coming for the blue flag".

Nathan groaned, "Who would believe that it was the Techonovans who made the first move this year"

"I pity their defenders; they are at a complete loss of position with two very powerful teams converging on them".

"The trouble in their paradise continues" Miles whistled, "The Techonovan Defenders don't seem happy with their Captain's decision."

"Yeah, but at least they comply. My guess is that their Captain must have asked them to defend against the Capers, while he himself guards the Flag against the Shaantilok"

Miles beamed, "Well, this seems like a blessing for Larry and Miguel. They now just have one giant between them and the flag".

Nathan returned his smile "Oh man, now this is funny" His face lightened up, "Does our man Larry thinks that the Techonovan Captain is in Junior Grade?" Larry tried to surprise the Techonovan Captain cum Flag Guard with his speed, but the big Defender was prepared. After a couple of fast swirls, when Larry resurfaced to take down the Defender, it was he who was surprised instead! A punch from that thick, hairy hand of the Techonovan Captain sent Larry down.

"You know Nathan, all this while, I thought Miguel had made a brave, yet calculated move by assuming the role of an Advancer" Miles' face remained expressionless, "But now I think, it is proving to be a fatal mistake.... But then, I can't blame him as well, they barely had any alternative"

Nathan looked at his fellow commentator with interest.

"I agree it's lost cause for Shaantilok" Miguel who was still in water, suddenly found himself amongst the sharks, there were so many of them now, and they seemed to have emerged out of nowhere. Left with no other choice, Miguel climbed up to face the huge Techonovan Captain.

"It's caper all over this year as well! Richa and Angelo, the two Techonovan Defenders are looking clueless with the mounting pressure from the Capers" Miles stared into the waters. He was right, although the other two Thechonovan Defenders were battling the Caper onslaught, but they seemed quite overpowered. "And not to forget Raj is there too" Miles had a frown in his voice, "But first things first, my bet is that Techonova will finish Shaantilok in less than a minute?"

The heavy Techonovan Captain swung into the action as soon as the Shaantilok Captain stepped on the blue platform. But Miguel was in no mood to go down as silently as Larry. When the big fist came for Miguel, Miguel dodged. Then replicating his opponent's action, Miguel too landed his fist deep into the Techonovan's flabby stomach. The big Techonovan swayed, his eyes scouting for his Shaantilok counterpart, who was already on his knees. The clinical scissor kick caught the Techonovan Captain on his calf. And the last hope for Techonova hit the ground, hard.

"Nathan, did you watch that?" Miles was practically screaming, "Did you just watch that, I mean Miguel was good, too good"

"Yeah," Nathan said, seriously, "He has not only managed to knock off the Techonovan Captain, but has also successfully blocked Raj"

"Exactly, the unconscious Techonovan Captain may be limp as a rock, now but his body is still big enough to stop Raj, even for those few vital seconds that Miguel can now use to recover the Techonovan flag"

"And he did it" It was Nathan's turn to thump his fist hard on the table in front, his face brimming with triumph, "Raj seems angry though," He chuckled, "someone tell him, it wasn't his fault, he was just strategically outplayed by Miguel."

Miguel flashed the blue flag valiantly. The Shaantilok's points tally flashed 80 points. Shaantilok was now just thirty points behind the Capers' total!

"Wait what?" Miles pushed Nathan by the back of his hand, as he stared at the Points Tally disapprovingly.

"What?"

"Look at the points tally. Eighty points!" Miles seemed stunned, "I don't understand, how did Shaantilok managed to gain so many points despite two major casualties and just one flag? Yea, Kumar earned some, but it wasn't more than five points or so. You has been playing behind the scenes for Shaantilok then?"

Even Nathan seemed confused as the fact dawned upon him, ultimately.

Down there in the water, Raj too had the exact same question.

=================================xxxxxxxxxxxxxxxxxxx=========================

Arjun had been missing from the battlefield for what seemed like eternity.

Beneath the water, unseen by all, he had been quietly navigating the treacherous waters for the last twenty minutes- battling of sharks and earning those fifty odd points in the process. But the battle was only growing intense- the sharks he had encountered until now were only minions. Now, he had entered the zone of huge hammer headed Shrogers- the actual guardians of the red flag platform.

Above, Miguel's mind was racing. With less than thirty minutes left in the match, Raj would definitely attack Shaantilok- it would be battle of great odds especially with Larry and Vijay already knocked out, and Arjun nowhere to be seen; it was now just six of them against the eight of Capers plus a Raj.

"Who do you think is taking home the Allakaadd this year?" Nathan asked, flashing a known smile.

"You actually expect me to guess?" Miles grinned.

But Miguel was wrong. Raj was busy elsewhere- his eyes scanning, searching the pool. Somewhere in these depths was a player who had been silently amassing points for Shaantilok. But who, or rather where was this ghost?

"Good move by Raj" Nathan remarked, "I think, he is aiming for new records this year." Giving quick directions to his teammates, Raj slowly swam towards the center. A few sharks tried to stop him, but he shoved them out of his way.

"Seems so" Miles agreed

"Forget that! Look at the waters" Nathan cried. Engaged in a fierce battle with Capers were the remaining Shaantilokians- it appeared like a lethal blend of arms' combat, and free style martial art, all happening at once between the two last standing contenders for the year's Allakaadd title.

"The Shaantilok team isn't that bad," Miles noted, "If you ask me, they and the Capers are pretty evenly matched, that of course is subject to Raj isn't in the equation"

"That's the difference. Raj changes everything"

"Oh my God!" Nathan exclaimed. "Did you see that?"

"What?"

"I swear I saw a small head surface from the water, but before I could take another look, it was gone" Nathan replied with a half stunned and half disappointed expression.

Miles was about to dismiss it as his imagination, when he saw Arjun resurface from the water, even though only for a second, "My God!" Miles raised his hands to his head in despair, "We are both idiots, both of us…. None of us noticed when that small boy from Shaantilok disappeared!"

Nathan' mouth pursed a little, "You mean that this small boy has been earning points for Shaantilok all this while?"

Miles sighed loudly.

Arjun had been spotted!

"You know what? Nathan muttered. "This is why Raj is after the red flag" Nathan remarked as Raj continued swimming towards the red flag.

"Was that Raj?" Nathan asked in surprise as Raj's cries filled the stadium

"Must be a Shroger attack" Miles observed, "It hurts!"

"I wonder if Raj will be able to continue after this severe attack"

"That's Raj, mate, not a human," Miles replied with a hint of insolence, "I think Raj is trying to fight off the Shroger" Indeed, Raj was putting every bit of his strength to kick the Shroger away, but the Shroger just wouldn't budge. In fact, it took Raj more than a few well-timed kicks to finally release the pressure as the limp Shroger floated away from him.

"Raj survives" Nathan sighed, "What's now?"

"It means the end of the Shaantilok" Miles sighed too; a sad, disappointed sigh, "Look up there," He pointed towards the Shaantilok platform, "The Capers' are pretty well using their surplus work force" He remarked, "And down here at the center, Raj is chasing that little boy"

"Almost everyone, except for Sigourney has been knocked out" Nathan frowned, "Even Sigourney is fighting against heavy odds"

"I feel bad for Sigourney" Miles said grimly, "She is a great friend. But right now, seeing her amidst punches and makes me feel bad"

"But where's Miguel?" Nathan asked, "I think, I just saw him a minute back"

"He was tactically thrown amongst the sharks" Miles replied, "Where he eventually perished under their mounting offensive"

"Even your worn out Shaantilok Defender finally falls into the water, Shaantilok flag is now for the Capers'" The Capers now had two of out of the three flags, and with the red flag too looking well within their reach this time, the Caper supporters could no longer hold back their cheers.

"I wonder, if we will ever see another team win?" Miles was still sad after what happened to his friend, Miguel.

"May be that day is today, I mean we cannot write off that young boy so soon" Nathan said, "He sure looked promising"

"With only ten minutes left in today's game, a mounting Caper attack, and over a fifty points' deficit, and you still believe the young boy from Shaantilok will be today's gamechanger, Nathan?" Miles sniggered.

In the water, Arjun, and Jovan Raj oblivious of everything outside, were slowly closing in towards the Red Flag, and barring the occasional Shrogers, it had all seemed under control till now.

The thunderous cheer made Arjun turn- Jovan was in his pursuit. But this short lapse of concentration proved to be fatal. As soon as Arjun dived underwater, he was hit by a runaway train, like his first day of training. The impact knocked the breath out of his lungs. Darkness slowly closed in. But, not now, not today. He strained his eyes, and his hands clawed at the water for something, anything to hold on to.

His hand gripped something rough.

A tail.

Summoning the last bit of his strength, he swung the massive blue Shroger by its tail- sending it crashing into the stands.

Panic erupted. The crowd screamed as the eight hundred pound beast landed inches away from the commentator's box. Paramedic immediately rushed to attend the wounded animal.

"What the hell?" Miles leaped off his chair. "Who did that?"

"That's my Shaantilok savior" Nathan chuckled. But no one noticed just how much that last action had drained Arjun.

And the battle wasn't over!

"Just in case you forgot, that savior of yours still has to fight the best Advancer of his time, and not forget his army that is quickly closing in from the other side"

"*Don't think.... Please don't think..... Just act Arjun...... Just act*" Arjun kept repeating to himself. With everything he was left with, he began one last ascent towards the red flag.

"Miles, I still think Shaantilok has an outside chance, if they can win the red flag" Nathan said, "With only a few feet left to be covered, and the last remaining Shroger already cornered by the Capers, it seems fate is finally smiling at the little boy"

"You wish" Miles jeered when Raj suddenly yanked Arjun by his leg, and his powerful fist went crashing into his little opponent's chest.

"The boy has at last been captured", Nathan spun on his chair in despair. "But why is Raj holding him by his neck instead of grabbing the red flag?"

"Maybe he wants to see this little boy who made it this far" Miles replied, and maybe he was right. But Arjun, barely conscious, made one last, desperate move- his fingers grazing Raj's eyes. Instinctively, Arjun was flung back. Raj's throw, even with one hand sent Arjun flying- straight into the flagpole. The whistle blew. A broken mast in his grip. The red cloth floating in the water.

The scoreboard flashed an extra hundred points for Shaantilok. The impossible had happened!

"That's my savoir pal, that's my savoir" Nathan jubilantly kissed Miles on his cheek, who was too stunned to even move away, just like those other thousand who stood speechless to this biggest upset. Shaantilok had won the Allakaadd and how!

"Ladies and Gentlemen" Nera Marshall held the microphone tightly between his moist fingers; his faces fighting hard to hide the obvious thrill, "What an evening this has been. I mean, the last time I remember someone winning a Red Flag was almost some thousand hundred years ago. Since that day we have waited for this day, and what a way it has come" his voice was trembling with each word, it had sure been an evening of unprecedented excitement, without any exceptions, "With countless casualties to his team, and being almost run down twice, a junior grader from Shaantilok brought it to its sixteenth ever Allakaadd title" An astounded audience stood silent, too stunned to even react "I congratulate Shaantilok for a stupendous show of teamwork, and strength today. Arjun Mehta, take a bow, you deserve it son; you deserve it thoroughly!"

"Arjun it is, then" Veera made a mental note.

On the stage, there was an obvious dismay. "Where's Arjun?" Was everybody's question

"In the infirmary" Nera Reran announced as he stepped to collect the Allakaad shield from Nera Brahmashiva.

"What happened?" Nera Marshall asked, his voice concerned.

"I am getting this feeling that this is how Arjun likes to celebrate every time he takes on a Shroger, or anything worse" Nera Reran replied, he had an assuring smile on his face.

X

The master of the five elements

"What a feat!" Nera Kashyap was ecstatic when he stepped into the Nera Supremo office.

Nera Brahmashiva smiled.

"What else do you need to believe that he is the reincarnation of the Mighty Vyom Vardhan?"

Nera Brahmashiva smiled again.

"What?"

"Don't jump to conclusions, Nera Kashyap" He said, taking a slow sip from his tall cup of hot chocolate, "The only way to confirm whether Arjun is the reincarnation of Vyom Vardhan is…."

"…..If all five elements grant him their powers" Nera Parvati restlessly groaned, "We know that Nera Brahmashiva Sir"

"And what about his extraordinary strength? Since the Mighty Vyom Vardhan, we have never seen a young Anvantara this powerful" Nera Kashyap shook his head.

"I admit his strength is remarkable" Nera Brahmashiva acknowledged, "but, he has to show signs of commanding the five elements."

"Why does it matter so much? Maybe he is different."

"Because Vyom wielded them all"

==============================XXXXXXXXXXXXXXXXXX=========================

It was his ninety-fifth day in the forests.

Thoris, once a towering figure of strength, now appeared beyond recognition. His overgrown bushy white beard and emaciated frame made him look thrice his age.

His patience was wearing off, yet for some reason he still clung to hope.

==============================XXXXXXXXXXXXXXXXXX=========================

"May I come in?" She knocked.

"Come in" Nera Brahmashiva replied. "Take a seat, Nera Kavya" He gestured towards the empty chair beside a worried looking Nera Parvati

"You wanted to meet?"

"Yes," Nera Brahmashiva said, his voice dark, "Arjun' whereabouts could be compromised any moment."

Nera Kavya leaned forward. "What happened, do we have a traitor amongst us?"

"Not just one" Nera Brahmashiva sighed; his expression grim. "The entire nature has turned against us".

Nera Kavya stared at him, surprised.

"Someone is using Faunatics to track him".

She frowned. "Faunatics?"

"An ancient Korean Tracking art. Basically, a Trackers uses animals and birds as their spies to find or track a subject" Nera Kashyap explained.

"I have never heard of it".

"Naturally" The Nera Supremo nodded. "It's a lost art".

She stiffened. "Who is reviving it now?"

"We still don't know. Right?" Nera Kashyap glanced at Nera Brahmashiva.

"Well," Nera Brahmashiva said, his voice slightly above a whisper, "That is why this council is here discuss. His name is Thoris".

"Thoris, General Thoris?" Nera Kashyap repeated, his voice laced with disbelief.

"Yes General Reoah Thoris. The highly decorated former general in King Hryiterehan's army".

"But why would he be after Arjun?"

Nera Brahmashiva eyes darkened further. "Ankara was his brother" A hush fell over the room "My Intel reports that Ankara is dead. Don't ask me how, but dead". His voice still barely a whisper, "I have reason to believe Tvashtar twisted the truth, making Thoris believe that Arjun is somehow responsible. And now, he is hunting Arjun to avenge his brother's death"

Nera Parvati studied his face, sensing something deeper. "That's not all, right?"

The Nera Supremo nodded. "Right, there's more".

The three pairs of eyes locked onto him.

"Well," Nera Brahmashiva continued, "Thoris and I have a history" He exhaled loudly. "We were once rivals."

"Rivals?" This time Nera Kavya asked.

He fell silent for a moment, lost in time.

"Yes, rivals. Back then our schools- Gurukule and the Anvantaras Institute often competed. Thoris and I were the leading champions and often contended against each other. I know this man too well. He is the most brutal fighter I have ever known. That is both his biggest weakness…. And his greatest strength"

The room grew heavy.

Nera Kavya was the first one to break the silence. "What options do we have?"

Nera Parvati clasped her fingers tightly. "Can we continue to hide him at Gurukule?"

Nera Brahmashiva shook his head. "Won't work! I don't think Gurukule can hold this secret for too long". Nera Brahmashiva turned to his west-facing window; his troubled gaze fixed on the snowcapped valleys beneath. "Send him to Africa with Miguel". He said at last.

"Who is Miguel?" Nera Parvati asked.

"The South African Defender from Shaantilok's Allakaadd Team" Nera Kavya replied.

Nera Kashyap lips parted. "But how does Miguel and Africa fit into all these?"

"The New Years is little over a month away. Although Miguel's father is a Portuguese, but his maternal grandfather still lives in Capone, a small Anvantara town near Nairobi. He is very well versed with African Jungle Battle Techniques- one of Thoris' preferred fight styles." The Nera Supremo turned towards his council of the three most trusted Neras, "That would buy us some time to think and plan".

"When should I arrange for his travels then?" Nera Parvati asked.

"Right away" He had no hesitation in his voice.

==============================XXXXXXXXXXXXXXXXXXX=========================

Mr. Natarajan returned earlier than planned and the boys wasted no time tracking him down, as soon as they got a whiff of this.

They finally caught him stepping out of Nera Norton's office. He greeted them. "Congratulations! I got the news."

Arjun responded with a quiet smile. The wait had been long, and their frustration was evident.

Sensing their eagerness, he smiled. "I know you are eager to complete your project, so let's get straight to it" Without hesitation, he stepped back into Nera Norton's office and settled into a chair. Nera Norton was out for his class and from the way Mr. Natarajan made himself comfortable, it was clear this wasn't his first time to Nera Norton's office, "So where were we?"

"Vyom Vardhan joined your West Command" Parth replied at once. He had scribbled everything on his notepad but didn't look at it once.

"Ah right" Mr. Natarajan nodded, "Over time our friendship grew stronger. Though he was many years younger than me, he was a hundred years wiser." He paused, his expressions darkening. "And, one day he received a call from the Vardhan Residence. I still remember we were in a meeting, and he hastily left... only to never return."

The boys exchanged glances. This cannot be the end of the story or was it?

"Did you guys lose touch after that?" Parth pressed.

"Not entirely." Mr. Natarajan smiled sensing his disappointment, "We stayed in touch through letters. It was through one of these that I learnt accidentally uncovered something extraordinary. He also mentioned he was going to the Himalayas to understand it better".

"The Himalayas?" Arjun asked, startled.

"Yes Himalayas. He wrote there was a great teacher who could help him".

"What was that extraordinary thing? Did he ever mention that to you?" Arjun asked.

Mr. Natarajan sighed. "No, he was always secretive about his life, but..." There was glint in his eyes, "But, I did some digging on my own" he laughed, "Vyom was training to command the five elements of nature".

"What five elements?" The boys again exchanged puzzled glances.

"The five fundamental forces of nature- Air, Earth, Fire, Sky and Water- the building blocks of the universe". He smiled at their innocuous faces, "Every particle of this creation is made of these five building blocks. The Five Elements encompass all that is needed to survive in this Creation. Without any one of the five, the universe would cease to exist."

"But how can air, water, sky, fire, earth help us?" Parth asked this time.

"Theoretically, Earth grants stability, Fire fuels positive energy, Sky offers healing, Water relieves stress, and Air brings calmness" Mr. Natarajan explained, "But for someone who has mastered all five elements, all relationship transforms- these five elements now give him power. So, earth cannot hurt, the water cannot drown, the sky cannot mislead, the air cannot sweep you away, and the fire can never burn. More than that, when wounded, these elements would heal you, and replenish your energy, if exhausted."

Parth's mind raced. "Is it possible for certain waters bodies to have natural healing properties?"

Mr. Natarajan's gaze sharpened. "No"

.

Parth hesitated before continuing, carefully choosing his words "But, if someone were to fall into water after being injured, and their wounds automatically heal, what would you say?" Arjun shot him a quizzical look; he clearly didn't know that his friend was referring to happened at the southern banks.

Mr. Natarajan didn't take his eyes off Parth, "I would say that the person has mastered the water element. Do you know someone like that?"

Parth forced a sheepish smile. "Just a thought" He lied. He wasn't ready voice his suspicion, not yet. Instead, he shifted the conversation. "So how long did it take for Vyom Vardhan to harness his powers?"

"Five Years"

===============================XXXXXXXXXXXXXXXXXX========================

Miguel peeked in her office, "You called for me, Nera Parvati?"

"Sit down, Miguel" Something in her tone made him uneasy. Unsure of what to expect, he pulled out a chair, "I hear you're heading to Kenya to visit your grandparents later this month" Nera Parvati said casually, her eyes studied him carefully.

Miguel frowned, "Is there a problem?"

Nera Parvati leaned forward slightly, "I just need a small favor".

Nera Parvati explained, her words measured. Parth, Santosh, Liam and Arjun had been assigned a winter project on African Jungle Battle Techniques, and Gurukule had reached out to Miguel's grandfather, Mr. Puolo Mangwa- an expert on the subject. And, Mr. Mangwa had agreed to mentor the boys, which meant the young boys would therefore be accompanying Miguel on his trip to Kenya. Miguel listened intently, though surprised at the mention of this connection between Grandfather and the Gurukule.

Meanwhile, in another office, Nera Michelle was handing out the project to the four boys. They kept exchanging glances throughout the conversation- unsure of why Miguel's grandfather was being assigned their project guide.

===============================XXXXXXXXXXXXXXXXXX==========================

The thrill of heading to a new country had Parth & Arjun buzzing, but beneath the excitement lurked a tingling uneasiness. The mystery of Mighty Vyom Vardhan still remained largely unaddressed and now trip this new project. There was something that they were unable to unravel.

"All set for Kenya guys?" Liam entered their room, noisily munching some chocolate chips.

"At least you of us is!" Arjun taunted playfully.

"More than ever" Santosh grinned as he joined the group, "By the way, I just ran into Miguel. He said we need to be at the Gurukule gate in ten minutes".

"No problem, we are ready to roll", Parth swung his backpack over his shoulder.

At the gate, a carriage was already waiting for them. "Where to lads?" The young driver smiled.

"Neranche Air pad" Miguel signaled the boys to hop in.

Waiting for them at the airstrip was an anxious Nera Barney, standing beside his prized flying machine. Unlike his usual laidback style, today he was dressed in the crisp white robes, "Get in Boys" He called over the roar of the engines.

Parth shielded his eyes from the wind. "Where are we headed, Nera Barney?" He tried to be as loud as possible

"Capone" Nera Barney yelled from the cockpit.

"No way" Miguel whistled, "You are taking us straight to Capone? I thought we were stopping at Nairobi".

Nera Barney grinned over his back, "What can I say, lad. It's your lucky day".

And, lucky they were, this just wasn't any aircraft- It was supersonic beast, built for speed over comfort. Hours could melt into minutes!

Now, it was just them, the sky and whatever awaited them at Kenya

==============================XXXXXXXXXXXXXXXXXXX=========================

Veera stood at the edge of her balcony, staring at the moonless sky. The Void was out there somewhere, a prison outside time itself. She knew what she had to do, but the *how* still eluded her.

Allakaadd had given her more than just a chance to observe the young Anvantaras, it had given her a name- Arjun.

Her father's sources at the school whispered troubling news. The Neras were planning to relocate Arjun- away from Gurukule, but why? What made him so important that they had to go to such extremes? Unmindfully, her fingers traced the ancient markings on the seal. There must be a way!

And then- she noticed it.

She lifted the seal and studied the delicate golden inscriptions intently- One phrase stood out *'Oasis of Shadows'*.

Every part of her mind told her this isn't a coincidence. Without wasting time, she turned on her heels and headed straight for the library.

It was an impressive library, though not as massive as Gurukule's. Its towering shelves cramped with forgotten knowledge- ancient literature and manuscripts, carefully preserved and passed down through generations of her family. And, somewhere in these weathered pages, there had to be something about the *oasis of shadows*- a clue, a hint, anything, just anything that could reveal the secret to unlocking the portal to breach the void.

Yet, the sheer volume of knowledge was overwhelming, a labyrinth of words and ancient wisdom. Finding the right piece of information felt like searching for a single needle in a haystack.

So, where to begin?

She carefully pulled out the seal from her satchel, scrutinizing it once more- there had to be more clues. There was nothing more beyond what she had already read. But then, her breath hitched- the word *shadows* had a faint, almost invisible glow. This had to be a clue, a signal- deciphering it though was another battle altogether.

Heart pounding, she wandered through the aisles- her eyes still glued to the seal.

As she passed a particular shelf, the glow on the word intensified.

This was it.

She immediately yanked book after book from the shelf, stacking the dusty manuscripts onto a nearby table. In the dim light of the library, she flipped through the brittle pages- ancient maps, battle techniques and lost arts.

The hours dragged on. Page after page, manuscript after manuscript, yet nothing definitive. It wasn't until the first ray of dawn steamed in through the high ceilings that she realized how much time had passed-she forcefully stifled a yawn. Exhausted, she quickly skimmed through the pages of another old book- nothing here as well. With a deep breath, she closed the book. She made a mental note to return in a few hours to restack the books back onto the shelf. As she began piling them one by one, her gaze caught a specific section of a lengthy epilogue etched into the binding of a worn-out book. She picked it up and read carefully- *The Oasis has many paths. The closest lies in plain sight yet, beyond the known world- hidden within a vast expanse where the western dunes whisper secrets and time bends to those who command the elements.*

Her breath quickened- Was it a desert? It wasn't just a metaphor- it was a fact. But where?

Instinctively, she traced her fingers lightly on the faded text, there were fine patterns, but she couldn't guess. Closing her eyes, she focused- and in that moment, the patterns yielded her the contours of Kenya's map.

================================XXXXXXXXXXXXXXXXXX=========================

Africa was nothing like any place they had been to. The biting cold was gone, replaced by warm heavy air that clung to their skin. Unlike snowcapped landscapes- sand dunes stretched into the horizon. The only white was a lonely cluster of clouds drifting lazily towards the distant plains.

"Where is Nera Barney?" A voice rich and weathered, cut through the moment.

An elderly African man stood before them- his thick brown lips and short scrubby white hair made him look like a treasure trove of lifetime's worth of stories.

"In the craft, grandpa" Miguel answered with a wide grin, stepping forward to embrace the old man.

Grandpa Mangwa faintly acknowledged the greeting, his gaze shifting to Nera Barney who was disembarking from the plane. "Miguel, take the boys to the van, I need a word with Nera Barney" He pointed towards a battered yellow van standing at the far end of the concrete runway.

"Long time Barney" Grandpa Mangwa greeted the pilot.

"How are you, my friend?" Nera Barney replied, shaking his hand with a light smile.

Grandpa Mangwa didn't smile. His expressions grave. "Nera Brahmashiva has sent a message, Barney. He wants me to train these boys- and he says it's urgent".

Nera Barney nodded, "Not just train them. You need to protect them too".

Grandpa Mangwa's frown deepened. "Yes, he mentioned that part as well. But I don't understand?"

Barney sighed. "Above my paygrade, mate. You know Nera Brahmashiva operates"

The old man studied him for a long time, before lowering his voice "At least tell me, Barney- Are the rumors true?"

He hesitated, then shook his head "Above my paygrade, mate. See you soon".

================================XXXXXXXXXXXXXXXXXX=========================

Half asleep, he fumbled for the bedside lamp, flickering it on with a groggy sigh "Yes?"

"It's me" The voice on the other end was low, deliberate.

Tvashtar's fingers tightened around the receiver. "I know it's you- General Thoris! What I don't know is why you are calling me at this hour". There was a clear frown in his voice

"The boy has been found".

His breath hitched. "Arjun?"

"Yes"

"Where is he?"

A brief silence. Then almost hesitantly whispered "Gurukule".

Tvashtar sat upright. "Gurukule?"

================================XXXXXXXXXXXXXXXXXX=========================

Her father would never allow such a journey. Not after knowing the consequences of her actions. But Veera had never been the one to follow the rules.

By nightfall, her plan was in motion. Dressed in a black cloak, her satchel with essentials, she booked the first flight to Nairobi.

One last glance at the towering Vardhan palace, Veera slipped into a waiting cab, unaware that her father stood quietly on a shadowed balcony above, his eyes following her.

The cool night air rushed against her face as she boarded the plane- towards the unknown.

Kenya awaited her. And with it the path that she was paving.

===========================XXXXXXXXXXXXXXXXXXX=========================

"*Jambo* (hello) boys, Welcome to Capone" A warm voice greeted them. An elderly, kind-looking African lady beamed at them a toothless grin. Her face was lined with years of wisdom and she wore her hair short, scrubby hair just as her husband, Grandpa Mangwa. "Miguel, take your friends upstairs. Let them freshen up before dinner". She instructed her grandson.

Miguel led them through the Mangwa villa. It was large, but somehow not large enough for the bustling family within. Excluding Miguel's, whose parents had settled in Portugal, the two sons, three daughters, and their ever-growing families, had every corner of the house brimming with life. The boys had to share a room, as all others were already filled to capacity.

Dinner to Mangwas, was no ordinary affair. It was a grand family gathering where everyone, from the youngest to the eldest, sat together on the floor to share a meal. It was an unbreakable tradition- and extended to everyone including guests.

The aroma of rich, spiced dishes filled the air as the feast began.

But only moments later, the Mangawas witnessed the first casualty. "Water, give me water" Liam gasped, his face contorted in distress as he pulled out a green chili from his mouth.

Miguel chuckled. "Grandma, *Maji* (water)"

His Grandma promptly poured a glass of water and handed it over to Liam with a kind, knowing smile.

Across the room, one of Miguel's bald, square-faced uncle let out a hearty laugh. "Your friends do not eat spicy food?" He teased.

Miguel smirked. "*Kidogo tu* (just a little bit)" He replied with a glint in his eyes.

===========================XXXXXXXXXXXXXXXXXXX=========================

General Kofi Raj was not in the best of moods. His jaws clenched, his boots furiously struck the polished floor as he impatiently paced his office- his eyes glued to his mobile phone. He was waiting, no rather expecting- it to ring.

An hour passed. Still nothing. His patience wore thin.

Restlessly, he picked up the intercom. "Jessie, send the Lieutenant in" He barked.

The door creaked open, as Lieutenant Sam Woods stepped into the office. It was the same young man who had been tailing Thoris from the Anvantara Institute,

"Yes Sir?" Lieutenant Woods delivered a crisp salute.

The General wasted no time. "Have you got hold of General Thoris yet?"

Lieutenant Woods hesitated. "My team is working on it, Sir"

General Kofi Raj frowned. "Any luck?"

Lieutenant Miles shook his head.

The General's nostrils flared up. "Not acceptable Sam! Fly over Nagvari" His voice boomed even outside the office. "Find me this man".

"Sure, Sir. I will leave first thing tomorrow morning"

The General's fist nearly slammed onto his desk. "Not tomorrow, not in the morning, not after the breakfast" His voice roared, his duck-like lips twitching furiously as he ordered. "I want you to leave right now. Find yourself a plane and just leave".

===========================XXXXXXXXXXXXXXXXXXX=========================

A small ground behind the Mangwa Villa had been chosen for their training.

When the boys arrived, Grandpa Mangwa was already warming up, stretching his arms and legs under the softy hue of the early morning sun.

"Boys, queue up." Grandpa Mangwa called out, his voice firm. They hurried into a line. "As you all know, for the next few weeks I will be teaching you the basics of African Jungle Battle Techniques." His gaze swept over their drowsy faces. "But before we begin, let me make one thing very clear- this is not something to be taken lightly. It is a demanding craft, and if you are not focused, you will fail."

The boys exchanged wary glances.

"Watch carefully" He continued "Each move I show you, you will have to repeat. African Jungle Battle Techniques is an ancient and primitive form of combat, where the fighter must rely on all their limbs- along with a few magic tricks- to outperform their opponents".

"Grandpa, how long does it take to master this art?" Miguel asked.

"The basics can be learnt in four to six weeks, but the advanced techniques- that could years- even a lifetime- depending on how far you wish to go".

"So, we're only learning the basics then?" This time, Arjun asked.

"For the most part" Grandpa Mangwa nodded, "But if time permits, I might teach you some Advanced Defensive maneuvers too". He looked at them, "So are you ready?"

"*Ndiyo* (Yes)" They chorused. It was the only Swahili word they had fully mastered.

Grandpa Mangwa smiled slightly before spreading his hands wide, slowly raising them into the air as he lightly bounced on his toes. The boys watched, intrigued. Then in the blink of an eye- he vanished.

"Here" His voice came from behind them. Spinning on their toes, they were met with the sight of Grandpa Mangwa standing right behind them, arms crossed.

Santosh, mouth fell open, "How did you do that? You were just in front of us a second ago".

"The technique is called *Bolaewal*- the trick of the wind" Grandpa Mangwa explained, "When you stand in the direction of the wind, you must throw your hands into the air, hold your breath and jump on your toes and the wind carries you wherever it's headed".

Santosh eagerly tried to repeat the move. He leaped into the air...and landed right where he started. "May be the wind has stopped!" He groaned.

Suppressing his smile, Grandpa Mangwa stepped closer, "No Santosh. You are doing it wrong. Hold your breath first- yes like that. Now raise your hands", He adjusted the boys palms, ensuring his fingers are evenly spread. "Now jump on your toes".

Santosh hesitated, then leaped. Seconds later, he was standing some four feet away from them. Liam whistled.

"My turn now" Arjun excitedly stepped forward. Grandpa Mangwa helped him too with the trick. Liam, Parth, and Miguel by then had understood the method; they all independently tried their luck. Miguel and Arjun were successful. But when it was Parth's turn, the trouble started!

Carefully following Grandpa Mangwa's instructions, Parth spread his palms; he double checked the position of his fingers, determined to not make the same mistake as Santosh. He took a deep breath and jumped.

But instead of Parth moving- the wind howled.

A sudden force surged through the air, hurling Grandpa Mangwa back into the trees!

==============================XXXXXXXXXXXXXXXXXXX=========================

"Looking for something?" A voice cut through the air as soon as the cab dropped her at Nairobi Hilton.

Veera turned sharply, her hand on the satchel, ready to sneak out her knife. Outside the gates of the imposing hotel, a man stood in the shadows, his arms crossed, a smirk playing on his lips.

"Depends on who is asking" She replied curtly.

"Someone who knows where you are headed. The Oasis, isn't it?"

Veera's grip tightened. "How do you know?"

The man stepped out of the shadows, revealing a weathered face and sharp eyes that had seen more than they should. "Because your father wanted to help you"

Veera's jaw dropped. "My Father? He knows I am here?"

The man nodded.

"But why would he send you?"

"Because I have been there" He said cooly.

==============================XXXXXXXXXXXXXXXXXXX=========================

The boys gasped.

Grandpa Mangwa pushed himself up, brushing the leaves and dirt off his clothes. "Where did you learn that, Parth?" He was fuming as he walked back, his expression dark.

Parth blinked in confusion. "Learn what?"

"*Nioewal*" Grandpa Mangwa said, his tone sharp.

"Nio what?"

"Don't play games with me, Parth" Grandpa Mangwa locked his eyes into Parth's. "This has to be the most lethal air attack in existence. If you had used just a bit more force, my body would have torn to pieces".

Parth paled. "I swear, I don't know what you are talking about! I did exactly what you told me to do".

"That's not possible, just not possible" Grandpa Mangwa muttered, shaking his head in disbelief, "Only the master of air can perform that move so flawlessly".

A tense silence.

Arjun looked at Parth; Parth looked back at him.

Were they both thinking the same thing?

================================XXXXXXXXXXXXXXXXXXX========================

She hesitated. This could well be a trap! Why would her father offer help without telling her? And yet, what if the risk is worth taking.

She despised moments like these- standing at the crossroads of uncertainty, torn between her caution and instincts.

She knew reaching out to her father wasn't an option- if it were, he wouldn't have chosen this way to helping her.

Unsure, she took a deep breath. "If you know the way, then take me there"

He titled his head, studying her with keen interest. "Very bold of you…. But, tell me- do you have the key"

"Key?"

"The one who commands all the elements of nature" He looked at her, amused. "You knew that already, didn't you?"

She sighed. "And that's the problem"

His gaze sharpened. "You don't know?"

"Not yet" She muttered in frustration.

A flicker crossed his eyes. "I have heard rumors" He admitted. "of the boy who moves beyond his age"

"Arjun from Gurukule?" She asked, her voice curious.

"Someone from Gurukule, yea" He confirmed.

"So that means I have to go back to Gurukule- then find and convince him" She groaned.

"Would he help?"

"I don't know" She confessed. "But I have no other choice." She studied him for a moment. "Are you coming with me?"

"He smirked. "No need" He said, leaning forward. "If rumors are true, your boy is in Gurukule anymore- he is in Kenya"

The man chuckled. "Kenya isn't just any place. It's also a test. And, if you are not ready, it will swallow you!"

"Then, let's find out" She challenged.

================================XXXXXXXXXXXXXXXXXXX========================

Kenya was becoming more than just a temporary stop- it was awakening. Each passing day brought new lessons, each more astonishing than the last. Under Grandpa Mangwa's watchful eyes, the boys learned both the techniques of survival and more about the fundamental secrets of the elements. They initially struggled through the grueling drills-summoning fire from thin air, jumping from daunting heights without scratch. Yet, it was the mysterious techniques that kept them on the edge- vanishing in plain sight, slicing through the air with kicks that defied gravity, and intricate web of offense and even some defense techniques that felt almost magical.

Parth like others, pushed himself in every lesson, his determination strong. Most of the times they went well, performing each move per instructions. But, during those rare occasions, when fire seemed to ripple or an impact carried power beyond explanation, Grandpa Mangwa would pause- his experienced eyes catching what the others missed. He never acknowledged it, dismissing those moments as Parth's reckless enthusiasm. Yet, deep down, he knew- the rumors were true, after all!

===============================XXXXXXXXXXXXXXXXXX=========================

"We should commence with the closest one" The man mused, running his fingers through his coarse beard.

Veera frowned. "What do you mean?"

He met her gaze. "There are about fifty, maybe fifty-five Anvantaras colonies scattered across Kenya"

She lifted her brows, a flicker of amusement appeared in her eyes.

He noticed. "What?"

"I just assumed less" She admitted sheepishly.

He sighed, clearly unimpressed. "Size isn't the issue" He grumbled. "Time is- I hope you know the Oasis of Shadows isn't accessible round the year"

That again caught her off-guard. "It's not?"

He shook his head. "It only reveals itself on the afternoon of the first full moon night of the first month- once a year"

A chill ran down her spine. "Then, we barely have time"

His gaze too darkened. "Barely"

===============================XXXXXXXXXXXXXXXXXX=========================

Miguel threw a pile of colorful African robes onto the bed, "Put these on" He grinned.

The boys eyed the garments warily.

"They are for the annual town festival today." He smiled, clearly enjoying their stunned expressions.

"You actually want us to wear these?" Arjun arched an eyebrow, poking at the robes as if they might bite

Miguel shrugged. "It's local dress code for celebration party after the annual swimming competition"

"Swimming competition?" Arjun repeated in a question.

Miguel nodded, then paused as a thought stuck him. His flickered with realization- most of these boys were ace swimmers- some like Arjun, after Allakaadd were practically legends in the water. "Why don't you guys compete?"

"I am in", Arjun said without hesitation.

"Me too" Parth agreed.

"I'll pass" Santosh said flatly, "Swimming isn't my thing".

All eyes turned to Liam. He scoffed. "What are you looking at? I am born to swim"

Dressed in their swimming trunks, the boys followed Miguel to the village river. The water deep enough for a good race, though the real challenge wasn't the depth- it was the crowd. The entire town had gathered, lining the banks eager to watch the most anticipated event of the year.

The course was two miles upstream, cutting through the hordes of competitors. The boys from Gurukule stood in the last row. Habituated to the enormous Jalsthal, they were finding it rather difficult to even move an inch without brushing against each other. In fact, they almost ran for the first quarter mile and as the water was shallow downstream, the others also weren't exactly keen on following the swimming etiquettes. It was only they progressed upstream and land steepened, the real race began.

One by one, contestants began dropping out- children, women, the elderly and those just for there for fun waded to the sidelines, cheering for the seasoned swimmers. But the boys from Gurukule pushed forward with relentless speed and precision. Well, most of them, Liam much to everyone's amusement, had already given up and was sitting beside Santosh "Maybe for once Liam feels at home" Santosh joked.

By the final stretch, only four swimmers remained- Parth, Arjun, Miguel and one enthusiastic local. Miguel was astonished- he had no idea Parth was such a good swimmer. But Parth knew his limits. His technique was strong, but endurance was another matter. His strokes started to slow, and he finally let himself drift back, onto a protruding rock at the bank to catch his breath.

Meanwhile, Arjun and Miguel were locked in a fierce battle for the lead. The crowd roared, chanting their names, though Miguel had the clear advantage of home support.

Parth, still panting at the riverbank, cursing himself for not training harder. But then...

The last remaining contestant collided straight into him; the impact was so powerful that it marginally knocked Parth back down into the water. His eyes dazzled as he came out of water, but rather than feeling tired and hurt, he was feeling refreshed. The sudden fall had accentuated his energy level, somehow.

It was time to test his theory.

Ahead, Miguel was desperately trying to keep up with Arjun, but his younger teammate from Shaantilok was simply unstoppable.

Then, just a few yards from the finish line, something zipped past Arjun- so fast, so precise, it might as well have been a bullet from the old revolver that that had signaled the start of the race.

Arjun's head shot up, his eyes wide with disbelief.

Standing at the finish line, ginning was Parth

The bird flying above screeched loudly and flew northwards.

===============================XXXXXXXXXXXXXXXXXXX========================

Resting on his bare, white-haired chest, the bird's fluttering wings stirred him to reality. Thoris blinked, his gaze meeting the sharp eyes of a brown-headed eagle. The bird screeched, jolting him upright. Without wasting a second, he gathered his belongings and rushed towards his once gleaming SUV- now barely recognizable covered in dust, bird droppings, and scattered leaves.

"Hello" he answered, fishing out his long forgotten solar powered phone from the rear seat.

"General Thoris?" came a familiar voice.

"Yes" The car lurched onto the smooth freeway with a dull thud.

"This is General Kofi Raj" The voice continued, "We have found Arjun".

"So have I" Thoris slammed his foot on the accelerator as he hastily swerved right, heading straight for New Delhi.

"You what?" General Kofi Raj crackled with disbelief, "Where are you now?"

"On my way to New Delhi. Next, first flight to Nairobi"

"Nairobi?" General Kofi Raj's confusion deepened.

"Where else did you expect me to go General?" Thoris asked sharply, eyes locked on the road ahead.

"To Gurukule?" General Kofi Raj replied, unsure.

"Why would I go to Gurukule when Arjun is in Kenya?" Thoris growled. How could Kofi Raj be so ill informed!

"Arjun is in Kenya?" General Kofi Raj's shock was palpable, "Who told you that?"

"An eagle"

"The what?"

"No time to explain General," Thoris' voice was curt. "I will call you if I need anything" Without waiting for a response, he tossed the phone out of the window. He needed to absolute focus, distractions irritated him.

=========================

The General stormed into the Throne Room, his temper flaring. "I told you this Thoris is nuts. He is heading to Kenya to find that boy. Kenya! Can you believe it? I told him Arjun is at Gurukule, but he wouldn't listen".

"To Kenya?" Tvashtar raised an eyebrow.

"Yes! And you won't believe why- he claims some bird told him Arjun is in Kenya" General scoffed, "The old man has completely lost it".

Tvashtar heaved a sigh of relief, "Ah! Faunatics, played its part then" He quickly filled his General in on the latest developments, leaving the general more bewildered than ever.

"Is that even possible?" The General's voice was laced with disbelief

===============================XXXXXXXXXXXXXXXXXXX========================

Exactly thirty-eight hours later- the young receptionist at Hilton Nairobi frowned at the sight of the ill-dressed, disheveled old man. His clothes were dusty and his hair unkempt. "You have a reservation, Sir?"

"Reoah Thoris"

She fed the name into her computer- Thoris was a *diamond* customer. She immediately broke into a professional smile, "Of course. A King Deluxe, Mr. Thoris, Welcome to Hilton Nairobi, Sir,"

Thoris had arrived in Kenya.

===================================XXXXXXXXXXXXXXXXXXXX========================
"Guys, be ready by seven tomorrow" Miguel peeped in. The boys barely reacted, sprawled out on their backs, their hands massaging their overstuffed stomachs- a consequence of indulging in annual day feast.

"Why?" Santosh mumbled, suppressing a yawn.

"Grandpa is taking us to Nairobi in the morning" Miguel replied, "So be ready"

Liam groaned, glancing at his watch. It was already past two in the morning.

===================================XXXXXXXXXXXXXXXXXXXX========================
It was the full moon night today. In the last two weeks every lead had been a dead end.

By the time they reached the sleepy little town of Capone, she had little hope left. As usual, the man had ventured into the town to ask about Arjun, leaving her to wait- again. She paced anxiously along the street, eager for the nearest coffee shop to open.

The streets were eerily deserted, most likely a hangover of the annual day earlier. she headed toward the coffee shop that had just rolling up its doors. - she bought a coffee, the warmth offering little comfort against her growing frustration.

The man was taking longer than usual. Maybe it's a bigger colony- she reasoned.

Minutes stretched into what felt like an eternity before he finally returned- he had a scrawny grin on his bearded face.

Veera narrowed her eyes. "What's with face?" She growled.

He chuckled. "Found your boy"

She blinked. "Here?"

"Not anymore. They left for Nairobi, an hour ago"

"Well, what are we waiting for?" She slid into the blue Fiat. "Lets go" She waited anxiously for the man to hit the accelerator.

He exhaled, gripping the wheel. "I have a feeling this will all be futile," he admitted, his voice laced with doubt.

She frowned. "What do you mean?"

"There's too much at stake. First, we need to find your boy. Second, we still don't even know if he commands all the elements. And even if he does, we have only a rather small window—between 12:00 and 12:30 PM today. I checked the planetary alignments. And even after that, we'll need all three of us to perform the ritual to breach the void- remember everything in those thirty minutes."

Her stomach twisted. "But we have to try, don't we?"

He hesitated before nodding. "Right." His grip on the wheel tightened. "Keep an eye out for an old yellow van," he muttered as the car hit the highway

===================================XXXXXXXXXXXXXXXXXXXX========================
The hotel phone was ringing madly just as Thoris stepped out of the shower.

"Mr. Thoris, your car has arrived" The voice from the other end informed.

For reasons he couldn't explain, the mention of the car made him freeze. A sudden weight settled in his legs, his heart pounding as a hammer. Was it the thrill of the hunt? The anticipation of finally closing in on his target. He couldn't tell. All he knew was that, whatever this feeling was, it made him nervous.

===================================XXXXXXXXXXXXXXXXXXXX========================
"How much longer?" Liam asked, stretching lazily in the back seat.

"Three more hours" Miguel replied.

"And what's on our agenda?" Santosh asked, hoping for something exciting.

"Simple- movies, lunch, parks?" Liam replied confidently.

"Wrong, the African Anvantaras museums" Grandpa Mangwa remarked from behind the wheel.

A wave of disappointment washed over the boys- not exactly the thrill they were hoping for

===================================XXXXXXXXXXXXXXXXXXXX========================
Capone lay a hundred and fifty miles south of Nairobi- Thoris observed on the GPS. He had already wasted months chasing the boy; there was no time to lose now.

"Can we go faster Grandpa Mangwa?" Liam groaned. The two hours on the road felt like an eternity.

"Just a few more hours, Liam" Miguel replied wearily. The cramped van barely fit the five boys, and the rough roads only made their journey more unbearable.

"Enough boys" Grandpa Mangwa pulled over for a break.

A small, untidy shack had an old, peeling Pepsi hoarding, precariously swaying above its battered roof. The shopkeeper, a wiry young man, didn't even care to spare a glance, too absorbed in the flickering black and white television set atop the counter.

"Why are we stopping now?" Arjun grumbled. They were exhausted and itching to reach the city.

"We are about cross the desert" Miguel explained. "This is the last shop before Nairobi. So grab, whatever you need"

"A coke for me" Liam said without hestitation.

Not far behind, Thoris' black hummer sped past old yellow van full of noisy boys. He had barely driven a few meters, when something in the rear-view mirror caught his eye- a brown eagle, gliding down, landing gracefully on the yellow van's roof. His grip on the wheel tightened.

===============================XXXXXXXXXXXXXXXXXXXX========================

Grandpa Mangwa barely had time to hit the brakes before the black Hummer swerved in front of the yellow van, coming to a screeching halt just inches away. Grandpa Mangwa's temper flared as he stepped out, his boots crunching against the loose gravel.

"What do you think you are doing Mister?" He growled, his eyes locked onto the stranger.

Thoris stepped out, unfazed. His pointed a finger towards the boys, his voice cold as ice. "Which one of them is Arjun"

Grandpa Mangwa froze. The question sent alarm bells ringing in his head. He straightened his spine, his voice measured, cautious. "There must have been some mistake. There is nobody by that name with us" He lied.

He had no idea who this man was, but he wasn't ready to risk the safety of the boys. Unfortunately, Thoris now knew the truth.

In one swift move, Thoris seized Grandpa Mangwa by the collar of his starched, blue shirt, and hurled him back. The impact sent Grandpa Mangwa crashing into the Hummer with enough force to make even the heavy vehicle move and then topple.

The boys sprang out at once, Miguel leading the pack. His thick biceps gleaming under the sun, "What was that?"

"Are you Arjun?" Thoris cut him off, his voice deadly calm.

Miguel clenched his fists. "No, but you are dead"

Thoris barely flinched. Instead he caught Miguel's incoming punch mid-air- and crushed his fist like a paper. Miguel's arm fell limp, his face wincing in pain.

The boys froze. Two of the strongest amongst them- had been taken in single moves.

Thoris' eyes swept over the boys once more. "Which one of you is Arjun?" He repeated.

There was a tense silence.

Arjun stepped forward. "I am"

Thoris' gaze darkened, as if every drop of blood in his body had rushed to his eyes. Without warning, his left leg shot out, aimed straight for Arjun's face. The boy raised both arms to block, absorbing the blow. But the impact was like Shroger hit. He somehow steadied himself, threw his hands into the air, and jumped. Thoris pulled him by neck from the behind, "Try those with someone your age" He hissed as his strong hand landed on Arjun's chin, this time it made contact. Another Shroger hit. His head was reeling, gathering the last bit of strength, Arjun drove his fist powerfully into the old man's stomach, but the old man seemed an expert of combat, he pulled back his stomach just in time, as his right knee went crashing into Arjun' chest, his mouth spurt blood.

Parth, Santosh, and Liam meanwhile were too focused on freeing Grandpa Mangwa from beneath the toppled Hummer, to even realize what was happening. they hadn't even noticed Arjun being on the receiving end of the old man's attack. They had assumed Arjun could handle himself- after all, he had done it so many times in the past. With Miguel almost crippled, the boys chouldn't let Grandpa Mangwa fend for himself under that heavy Hummer.

Their Anvantara strength was nothing short of extraordinary. Together, the three young boys helped Grandpa Mangwa up. "Boys, you have to leave" Grandpa Mangwa said in a trembling voice, "Go to the village and get help. This man is beyond us".

"We are not leaving without you" The boys replied adamantly.

Just a few meters away, Arjun was locked in a losing battle. It was unlike anything he had faced before. He survived the crocodile in Nagvari, bested Nera Vesper in Gurkule, outperformed his schoolmates while handling sharks and even stood his ground against the massive piorotaur. Yet, none of it mattered now. Finding it increasingly impossible to match up to the might of Thoris. With each blow, Arjun was losing bits of his consciousness.

The last jab brought the boy down completely- almost unconscious and terribly out of breath.

Thoris seized the moment to draw a gleaming sword from a sheath hidden beneath his black coat.

He raised it over Arjun and swung it viciously.

XI

The final battle

But, before the blade could make contact, something extraordinary happened. As if propelled by an unseen force, the sword was ripped from Thoris's grip and sent spiraling away like a feather in the wind.

"Looking for this" Santosh asked. balancing Thoris's sword delicately on the edge of thin long rod that he held between his fingers.

Thoris yanked the sword back. "Stop me if you can, lad"

Without hesitation, Santosh met the strike; countering the attack from behind as Thoris used the air defense technique. In a rather swift motion, Santosh spun on his heels, sweeping his blade toward Thoris. But the seasoned warrior blocked it with ease, his though sharp eyes admired the boy's craft.

"Who taught you fencing?" Thoris inquired, slashing at Santosh's neck.

Santosh deflected the strike mid-air, "My father".

Just as their battle was reaching its peak, Thoris exhaled a small cloud of dust. The vigilant young boy swiftly dodged—but he failed to notice the hidden blade within that dust storm. Thoris's sword clipped the rod from Santosh's grip, and in the very next moment, the heavy handle of his sword slammed into the boy's skull. The world blurred as Santosh collapsed, unconscious. Thoris angrily held his sword at Santosh's neck, trying to decide what to do with this young boy. Unsure, he swung the sword.

Before the blade could connect, it was whisked away, once again.

"Not again" Thoris groaned, his patience wearing thin. "Enough of these petty air tricks, you old buffoon"

Thoris rubbed his hands together, generating a huge firball.

Grandpa Mangwa recognized the move, and swiftly aside, as a huge fireball whizzed past him.

"Old trick, man" Grandpa Mangwa taunted, knowing fully well that distracting Thoris was the only way to buy the boys some time. He prayed for help to arrive before it was late.

Thoris sneered. "Fine. How about this, 'man'?" Thoris stomped the ground hard, triggering a tremor that rattled the earth.

The attack took Grandpa Mangwa by surprise. He lost his footing and fell backwards- just in time for another fireball to come hurling towards him. Grandpa Mangwa would have been cooked by the blaze hadn't Parth put his hand just in time to block the fireball. Parth felt an odd, cold sensation as the fire touched him.

"Run. I will try to divert his attention" Grandpa Mangwa whispered urgently, as he pulled himself up. Parth nodded as he watched the elderly men engage in a fierce duel of fireballs.

Grandpa Mangwa had seen the fireball trick too many times to be deceived by it—but Thoris wasn't relying on simple tactics. He was weaving the fireball technique with the infamous air spoon trick, creating a devastating combination. First, a sudden gust of air would hurl the opponent backward, throwing them off balance, and before they could recover, the fireball would strike with merciless precision.

Thoris unleashed this relentless assault, his movements calculated, his steps closing in on Grandpa Mangwa with every attack. Not only were his strikes growing fiercer, but the gap between them was shrinking as well.

Meanwhile, time was slipping away for Parth. Arjun was unconscious. So, was Santosh. Miguel was crippled. And Liam? Liam would have been paralyzed with fear. But could he be blamed? Expecting a boy who was terrified of Manuel—a classmate—to stand against an assassin like Thoris was sheer madness.

Grandpa Mangwa was fighting valiantly to hold his ground against the relentless onslaught from Thoris. Yet, despite the assassin closed in, now mere foot away "Dasvidaniya old man" Thoris hissed, releasing another fireball. Grandpa Mangwa's half burnt body slammed into the now abandoned shop, the impact sending splinters of wood and dust flying.

"Where do you think you are taking that boy?" Thoris snarled, he had spotted Liam hauling Arjun over his shoulder, making a run for the van—Liam had somehow stealthily been able to push through the field without drawing attention.

"Away from you!" Liam shot back defiantly. His voice wavered but he refused to show fear. Even Parth gaped at his friend's stupid heroics.

"Then shall we see how fast you are?" Thoris jeered.

"Faster than you will ever be" Liam retorted.

Parth realized Liam was stalling, trying to buy time. But for what? Neither of them knew.

To their surprise, Thoris even let Liam run.

There was a gentle tap on Liam's shoulder, followed by a powerful punch to his right temple. Liam crumpled instantly, unconscious, Arjun too tumbled from his grasp, landing lifelessly on the ground. Thoris had tricked him—an invisible strike, perfectly executed

"Enough of this" Parth lunged, locking his legs around Thoris' shoulder, twisting his neck. Then deftly dropping himself behind Thoris' tall legs, he flipped the assassin over his back, sending him crashing to the ground. Without hesitation, he wrapped his legs around Thoris's arm, attempting to snap it in an arm-breaker.

But Thoris wasn't done.

With a brutal yank, he tore Parth off him and hurled the boy over his shoulder. Parth fell on his back- a drop of saliva trickled down his dry mouth.

But Thoris wasn't done. He retrieved his sword from the ground and swung it at the little boy. Instinctively, Parth raised his arm to shield himself.

The steel met skin.

The blade broke.

Thoris stepped back in disbelief- The boy lay there, without a scratch.

Baffled, he drove his fist into Parth' chest; the attack took Parth by surprise, giving him no time to react, as Thoris grabbed the young boy by the collar, and tossed furiously him into the air.

Meanwhile, his free hand generated a massive fireball and aimed at the dry hay that was stacked next to the shop. The flames erupted, turning the hay into an inferno. And, Parth landed straight into it!

===============================XXXXXXXXXXXXXXXXXXX=========================

"There!" She screamed.

The man looked at her quizzically, "What?" His foot slammed the breaks.

"The yellow van"

They rushed out of the car at once. What they saw they weren't expecting!

A tall, old man in black suit was watched in fulfillment as a small, trembling hand emerged from the raging fire- only to retreat back into the searing flames. Around the van, three bodies lay scattered, each bearing a wound of varying degrees of severity. At Grandpa Mangwa's urgent urging, Miguel had somehow slipped away, racing against time to find help.

"What happened here?" The man scanned in disbelief. "And any of them is your boy"

Veera swallowed hard. "The one over there" Veera pointed at Arjun lying unconscious on the field, his white shirt stained red with blood and dust.

Thoris stood nearby, his chest rising and falling with heavy breaths. His sharp eyes too scanning the fields. A strange sense of satisfaction flickered in his eyes. Everything was falling into place- every obstacle had been uprooted.

Thoris took his time to bent down and retrieve the rod he had clipped off Santosh and turned back to where Arjun lay.

"Vengeance". He growled, "I have avenged you Ankara, I have avenged you my brother". He howled, his eyes looking heavenwards. But, this was not the same man who had mercilessly beaten most of them moments ago. This man looked... different. Older. Weaker. A grieving brother carrying the weight of his loss.

He raised the rod with both his hands and aimed for Arjun' head. *The boys must not survive* he reminded himself.

Veera and the man watched from far, immobilized completely by the turn of events- watching the scene unfold in horror.

"Arjun didn't kill your brother" A voice rang out.

Thoris stiffened. His breath hitched. "That's impossible," he muttered, shaking his head. "Impossible."

Veera too rubbed her eyes in disbelief.

A young boy had stepped out from the fire, unhurt.

"It wasn't Arjun who killed Ankara," Parth continued. "It was Ankara who murdered Arjun's parents in Nagvari." the voice from Kavya's phone echoed in his ears. He now knew what it really meant about *Tracker Ankara.*

Parth took a step forward, his gaze steady. "Sir, you have to believe me," he said, addressing Thoris with unexpected respect. He had seen the pain in the old man's eyes. "Arjun was with me in Mumbai when your brother murdered his parents. He was always in Mumbai. You've been misled, sir."

"Lies!" Thoris bellowed, his voice laced with rage. His hands trembled as he covered his face, his body quivering with grief, fury, and disbelief- all at once. He looked up—slowly, painfully—his eyes ablaze with hatred. "It's a lie! I *know* it's a lie!"

With a furious snarl, he hurled a massive fireball at Parth.

But Parth caught it.

His fingers curled in response, and with a flick of his wrist, he sent a powerful gust of wind surging toward Thoris, knocking him backward.

Parth hadn't wanted to fight back. But he understood—the old man needed to vent his anger, needed an outlet for his pain.

Thoris staggered to his feet, his body rattled not just by the impact, but by something far more terrifying—his own misjudgment. He clenched his jaw and slammed his foot into the ground.

The earth trembled violently.

But Parth remained unfazed. The ground beneath him didn't even shift.

Then, in perfect defiance, Parth stomped his own foot. The earth shattered beneath Thoris. The assassin fell backward, his body crashing hard onto the dust.

His wide, disbelieving eyes stared up at Parth. "Tell me this isn't real," he gasped. "Tell me this is a lie. Tell me you are *not* the reincarnation of Vyom Vardhan. Tell me you are not the master of the five elements!"

Parth sighed. "Honestly, I really don't know."

"No one—*no one*—on this earth can control all five elements except Vyom Vardhan," Thoris murmured, his voice distant, haunted. "And *he is dead*. I *saw* him die before my very eyes." His breath quickened, his chest rising and falling in uneven bursts. "I was there when Tvashtar slit his throat with his sword" His face darkening, his expression unreadable, "I was there when Advisor Vardhan was drowned in the blood of his own son," he whispered, his voice hollow. "I *was there* for all of it."

Parth's fingers twitched. Disgust churned in his gut. He had no memories of whatever Thoris was talking about, no recollection of Vyom Vardhan or the horrors the assassin described. But the words alone were enough to make his stomach churn. His hands clenched into fists, and without realizing it, he unleashed another powerful gust of wind.

Thoris didn't even try to dodge. He lay there, his eyes distant, his face unreadable.

Parth wasn't sure if Thoris was speaking the truth, trying to enrage him, or simply unraveling under the weight of his own memories. But one thing was certain—he now felt nothing but repulsion for the man before him.

Thoris let out a low, guttural laugh. "No matter what you do, you can't kill me," he said, his voice dripping with malice. His fingers twitched behind his back, working subtly, discreetly. "You died then... and you will die now."

Too late.

A massive fireball erupted from Thoris's hands. Parth was too late to register.

Instinct took over. Without even thinking, this time Veera countered with one of her own. She had to save him- Parth was her key.

The two fireballs tore through the air, colliding into their targets with explosive force.

Thoris crumpled, his body contorting as the flames seared through him. The stench of burning flesh filled the air.

But, this time, Parth was not unhurt. Yet, this fireball... it wasn't *hot*.

It was *cold*.

It seeped into his skin like a damp, rotting cloak, choking him, suffocating him. His vision blurred. His breath hitched.

Darkness.

Somewhere, in the distance, he saw them.

His parents.

His sisters.

Jignesh, Vibha, Sara... and Arjun.

They stood together, waving, calling out to him.

The smirk returned to his bearded face as he watched Veera rush to Parth. "The rumours are real, after all."

Epilogue

Pangong Lake, Ladakh, India

The night thickened. The barren, rocky stretch of land near the Pangong Lake was now almost swallowed by the encroaching fog, its heavy veil obscuring everything, everyone in sight.

A lone figure emerged from the mist- his silhouette sharp against the moonlight glow. His eyes piercing the thick fog as he approached the solitary cabin, like an outpost lost in the rugged wilderness.

"Got a light, mate?" His voice was smooth, almost amused.

The guard, bundled in layers against the cold, struck a match. The tiny flame flickered, casting shadows over the stranger's face. A sharp inhale. The match dropped. Horror widened the guard's eyes. He knew that face. That was impossible. That man was dead.

"You?" The word escaped in a whisper.

"Yeah, me." The stranger's hand struck fast, a lethal blow through the night. The guard's body crumpled, lifeless.

A voice from inside shattered the quiet. "Who's there?"

The unknown man at the door stepped inside. In the flickering bulb overhead, a man slouched in an armchair, bottle in hand—General Mohith Natarajan, once a feared warrior, now a remnant of his former self.

The years had not been kind. His sharp features had softened into folds, his once-powerful frame dulled by time and drink. He squinted at the intruder with a wide disbelief on his face.

"You?" His voice wavered. "How... how are you alive?"

"Not happy to see me?" the man asked, a cruel smirk playing on his lips.

"B-but... Tvashtar killed you. I saw it with my own eyes!"

"Did you, Natarajan?" The man tilted his head.

Panic flickered in the old General's gaze as he darted glances across the room, searching for a weapon, an escape. Anything.

"Don't even think about it," the man warned. A heavy knife landed with a thud on the table- between Natarajan's trembling hand and the pistol lying inches away. "And in case you're waiting for your men... they're not coming. They're all dead."

"You killed them? All of them?" Natarajan's voice cracked.

"What do you want?"

"Where is Tvashtar?"

The name alone sent a shudder through Natarajan.

"I don't know."

The visitor's patience snapped. His heavy foot connected with Natarajan's chest, sending him sprawling onto the wooden floor. The chair shattered beneath him. He gasped for breath.

"I *don't* know," he groaned.

"Who does?"

"The Neras," Natarajan stammered. "Or... or Khan. He's General Kofi Raj's top spy in Asia."

"Khan?"

Natarajan nodded weakly.

"Where do I find him?"

"Tashkent, Uzbekistan. He owns a hotel in Amir Temur Square."

"That all you got?"

"I swear it."

The man studied Natarajan for a moment. Then, gently, he helped the General back to his seat.

"I liked you, Natarajan, you were my friend once" he murmured, his grip tightening on the old soldier's shoulder. "But... I wish you hadn't followed the king's orders that day."

A sharp movement- a muffled gasp. The flickering bulb trembled, casting monstrous shadows as Natarajan's lifeless body slumped forward.

===============================xXXXXXXXXXXXXXXXXXXXXX========================

Tashkent, Uzbekistan (2 days later)

The door creaked open. A young boy stepped out. He barely looked up from the Facebook page on his phone. "Yes?"

"I need to see Khan."

"And you are?"

"Tell him General Kofi Raj sent me."

Minutes later, Khan appeared. His off-white shirt clung loosely to his frame, his hair dishevelled, he supressed a yawn as he stared at the man.

"You work for General Kofi Raj?" His voice has a subtle hint of suspicion.

"Yes."

Khan's gaze swept over the visitor. "Strange. His men are usually... better dressed."

The man laughed. "The ponytail's bothering you, huh?"

Khan smirked. "It does seem a little out of place."

"That's because I don't work for General Kofi Raj."

Khan's smile faded. "Then who are you?"

The man stepped closer. "Vyom Vardhan." He whispered coldly.